Please return/renew this item by the
last date shown to avoid a charge.
Books may also be renewed by phone
and Internet. May not be renewed if
required by another reader.

www.libraries.barnet.gov.uk

B A R N E T
LONDON BOROUGH

MONSTER HIGH

GHOULFRIENDS
just want to have fun

WRITTEN BY
GITTY DANESHVARI

ILLUSTRATED BY
DARKO DORDEVIC

L B

LITTLE, BROWN BOOKS FOR YOUNG READERS
LBKIDS.CO.UK

LITTLE, BROWN BOOKS FOR YOUNG READERS

First published in the United States in 2013 by Little, Brown and Company
First published in Great Britain in 2013 by Little, Brown Books for Young Readers

Copyright © 2013 by Mattel, Inc. All rights reserved.
MONSTER HIGH and associated trademarks are owned by
and used under license from Mattel, Inc.

Special thanks to Emily Kelly and Darren Sander
Spot art by Chuck Gonzales

The moral right of the author has been asserted.

A CIP catalogue record for this book
is available from the British Library.

ISBN 978-0-349-00122-7

Printed and bound in Great Britain by
Clays Ltd, St Ives plc

Papers used by LBYR are from well-managed forests
and other responsible sources.

MIX
Paper from
responsible sources
FSC® C104740

Little, Brown Books for Young Readers
An imprint of
Little, Brown Book Group
100 Victoria Embankment
London EC4Y 0DY

An Hachette UK Company
www.hachette.co.uk

www.lbkids.co.uk

For Brooklyn's newest monsters,
Ronan and Emmett

CHAPTER one

Unfettered by even the faintest wisp of cloud, a large wrought-iron gate shimmered brightly in the sunshine. The landscape was empty and eerily still, save for a few silky spider threads fluttering around the spindly black bars. Looming in the distance, just behind the fence, was the Gothic window–filled facade of Monster High. And though everything appeared just as bright and cheerful as it always did, something ominous lingered in the air— something that hinted at unfinished business.

Three shadows crept slowly toward the gate,

instantly altering the barren landscape. Distorted by the sun, their arms, legs, and torsos morphed in and out of carnival-mirror caricatures. Breaking away from the pack, a long and sinewy arm reached for the fence, wrapping five fingers tightly around the bars.

"Ouch!" Venus McFlytrap screeched as she quickly released her hand from the gate. "Can someone please explain why we're down here so early? My vines haven't even woken up yet," she grumbled, rife with attitude, before stifling a yawn.

The emerald-skinned daughter of the plant monster then draped her long pink-and-green-striped hair over her pet potted plant, Chewlian. Much like a curtain, it shielded him from the blazing sun.

"Poor Chewy. I think his leaves are wilting," Venus said as she tenderly watched him snap at a passing gnat. "Well, at least the heat hasn't affected his appetite."

"*C'est très important* that I never mislead anyone. Therefore, I would like to preface this statement by reminding you that I am neither a trained botanist nor a horticulturist," Rochelle Goyle explained formally in her charming Scarisian accent.

"Seriously, Rochelle?" Venus replied with a roll of her eyes. "The odds of me mistaking you for a botanist or a horticulturist are zero. Actually less than zero."

"Very well then. Have you considered applying sunscream to Chewy's leaves? I think SPF thirty could do wonders for him. If I were not carved from granite, I would wear it dutifully."

Though crafted from stone, Rochelle was a surprisingly dainty gargoyle with small wings that crowned just above her shoulders. And ever the style maven, she always found new and inventive ways to repurpose accessories. On this particular day, she had arranged her long pink hair with teal-streaked bangs in a bun using a yellow Scaremès scarf to hold it in place.

"Deary me, if ever I felt like a bat on a hot tin roof, it's today. Why, it's absolutely *steaming* out here!" blue-and-black-haired Robecca Steam exclaimed in her usual overexcited manner.

"Technically speaking, it's not actually steaming out today," Rochelle stated authoritatively before raising her eyebrows. "I thought you of all ghouls would know that."

Fashioned out of a steam engine by her mad-scientist father, Hexicah Steam, copper-plated Robecca came with both bolts and gears. And though she was built ages ago, she had been dismantled for quite some time and had only recently been put back together. Not that anyone could tell: Robecca was absolutely perfect—or, rather, *almost* perfect. Burdened with a highly unreliable internal clock, she was incapable of arriving anywhere on time. And so it fell to her friends to keep her on schedule or, at the very least, vaguely aware of the hour.

"Rochelle, I hate to be a thorn in your side, but why did you drag us down here so early? It's almost like we put *you know who* in charge of watching the time," Venus said while motioning conspicuously in Robecca's direction.

"Isn't this just the bee's knees? I'm a *you know who*! I've always wanted to be a *you know who*, because everyone knows that anyone who's anyone is a *you know who*!" Robecca sounded off exuberantly.

The copper-plated ghoul then switched on her rocket boots and performed a quick backflip in the air.

"Robecca, I hardly think that warrants a celebration," Venus said drily as she turned her gaze back to Rochelle. "Well?"

"I must agree: Aerial maneuvers can be *très dangereux*. Consequently, I suggest refraining from them unless absolutely necessary."

"Rochelle! Forget about Robecca's aerial maneuvers! What's this morning's plan? Why did you insist on getting us down here so early?" Venus snapped as something dashed between her pink boots. "Ugh, Roux! Give it a rest; your enthusiasm is starting to irritate me."

"I think it's high time Roux tried out for Fearleading. I mean, just look at her—she's a natural," Robecca teased Rochelle playfully.

Roux, Rochelle's pet griffin, was perpetually happy, at times almost annoyingly so. It was as

though the small winged creature could not experience any other emotion. In many ways she was the polar opposite of Robecca's mechanical pet penguin. Whereas Roux was always happy, Penny was always grumpy. But then again, Robecca did have the most tiresome habit of accidentally leaving her places. Over the past few months Penny had been left everywhere—from a public restroom at the Maul to the frozen-foods aisle at the grocery store, neither of which could be considered a mechanical penguin's natural habitat.

"Rochelle, are you going to tell me the plan or what?" Venus griped as she pushed back her vines to theatrically check her watch.

"Paragraph 6.8 of the Gargoyle Code of Ethics states, *en detail*, that a gargoyle must abide by his or her word. And I gave Skelita Calaveras and

Jinafire Long my word that I would be their tour guide on their first day at Monster High."

"I really am as keen as a jelly bean to meet your new friends. If only Venus and I could have gone on the trip to Scaris, then they'd be our friends too," Robecca buzzed as she turned to look at Penny, whose left wing was emitting a slight squeak as it flapped. "I think it's time for someone to get an oil change at Grind 'n' Gears."

While the sun continued to shine brightly, the three ghouls lapsed into silence, their minds drifting to the many things that lay ahead. First to the excitement of seeing old friends, then to the homework they were soon to be burdened with, and finally to the still-unexplained monster whisper.

Never one to keep something to herself, Robecca abruptly squawked, breaking the silence. "Eek! I can't stop thinking about Signore Vitriola's warning! Do you think he was right? Will those responsible for the whisper soon return? Oh, just the thought of it makes me want to blow a gasket!"

"Robecca, *s'il ghoul plaît*, you mustn't blow a gasket so early in the day. Though, I understand the feeling. It certainly was a precarious time with the students and faculty unable to think for themselves," Rochelle remembered somberly.

"Ghouls, you're missing the point. It's not about whether those responsible will return; it's whether they ever left," Venus stated pointedly.

"Are you referring to Madame Flapper?" Rochelle questioned Venus while cradling Roux in her arms and rocking him, much to the petite creature's delight.

"I just don't know if I believe Miss Flapper's story. I mean, you have to admit it's pretty convenient. She claims she was under a spell too, erasing any and all responsibility for brainwashing the school," Venus answered, absolutely bristling with suspicion.

"But what about the way Miss Flapper reacted when she heard what she had done? She was devastated," Robecca recalled.

"Um, hello! She was acting." Venus scoffed, shaking her head at her ghoulfriend's naïveté.

"Good golly. If that's true, she's one heck of an actress. Maybe even better than Feral Streak!" Robecca remarked with astonishment.

"At this point it's impossible for any of us to say for sure whether Miss Flapper was in fact behind the whisper or simply another one of its casualties. And for that reason, we must keep our eyes open at all times. Except of course if something sharp is careening toward our heads or if we're sleeping," Rochelle clarified earnestly as Venus and Robecca stifled laughter.

"Hey, ghouls, talk about the early birds catching the worm," casually clad sea creature Lagoona Blue called out in her Mosstrailian accent as her sometimes boyfriend, Gil Webber, scampered up behind her.

"Lagoona! Gil!" Venus, Robecca, and Rochelle greeted the couple warmly, pleased that the hour had finally come for the school day to begin.

"Morning, mates!" Lagoona said warmly. "Say, Venus, did you get my e-mail about the oil spill?"

"Ugh, those careless cretins make me so angry! I wish I could pollinate every single one of them!" Venus huffed furiously, thinking of how helpful her pollens of persuasion could be in convincing greedy oilmen to take better care of the ocean.

"*Boo-la-la*, Venus," Rochelle remarked. "You mustn't get so upset. You're turning red, which is not a good thing for someone who is supposed to be green."

"She's right, mate. The only way to help the environment is to keep calm and swim on," Lagoona concurred before she and Gil joined a slow-moving pack of zombies en route to the entrance to Monster High.

"Nice updo, Rochelle!" a beautifully coiffed werewolf exclaimed while sashaying past the trio.

"*Merci boo-coup*, Clawdeen," Rochelle gushed, proudly patting her bun still held neatly in place with the bright yellow scarf.

"Gee whiz, did you get a gander at Clawdeen? The hair, the clothes, the pearly-white fangs—she's the absolute, the cat's meow," Robecca mused as she watched the ghoul strut confidently away in purple wedge sneakers.

"Did someone say *fangs*?" Draculaura, the daughter of Dracula, asked with a wink.

The fair-skinned ghoul with pink-and-black-striped hair then lifted the straw in her iron shake to her perfectly glossed mouth. As a vegetarian vampire, she had no choice but to supplement her diet with iron shakes. Fortunately she had long ago learned how to sip without smudging her lipstick.

"Hey, Draculaura!" Robecca thundered happily as Venus and Rochelle waved hello.

"Ghouls," Draculaura said, squinting in the bright light. "I'd love to stop and chat, but this sun is definitely not vampire-friendly."

"Tell me about it. My bolts are burning up," Frankie Stein, the gorgeously mint-green daughter of Frankenstein, interjected as she stepped out from behind a passing werewolf.

"Wow, Frankie, nice stitches," Draculaura noted with an approving nod.

"Thanks. I had to stay up all night sewing, but it was worth it to look voltage for the first day back," Frankie replied as she and Draculaura continued walking together toward the main entrance to Monster High.

"Oh great," Venus whined sarcastically. "Get ready to curtsy. Royalty's approaching."

Dressed in opulent gold bandages and a shimmering jeweled headdress, Cleo de Nile was rather hard to miss, especially with her handsome boyfriend, Deuce Gorgon, following close behind. Their romance was proof positive that opposites really do attract. For where Cleo was extraordinarily demanding, to put it nicely, Deuce was laid-back and easygoing.

"Hey, Rochelle," Deuce greeted the blushing gargoyle amiably, inciting a stampede of butterflies through her stomach. "Robecca, Venus, how are you ghouls?"

"Deuce? The sun is really hot, sort of like me," Cleo interrupted as she reached out, grabbed his arm, and pulled him along. "We need to get inside before my eyelashes melt off."

Mere seconds after they escaped earshot, Venus turned to Rochelle with a raised eyebrow and a knowing smirk. "Crush much?"

"As you are well aware, I am no longer with Garrott DuRoque; however, that does not change the fact that Deuce is still very much with Cleo, and per the Gargoyle Code of Ethics—"

"Save your citation. We get the drift," Venus interjected as her body tensed and her vines fluttered at the

sight of a sleek orange werecat approaching.

Sauntering toward the gate was Monster High's most notoriously difficult pupil: the stripe-faced and perky-eared Toralei Stripe.

"Was that Cleo?" she purred, seamlessly blending judgment and disdain as she flicked her fur forelock away from the dark orange spot surrounding her left eye. "I thought I smelled something."

"Cleo is a bit of a perfumista. Rumor has it she has a different scent for each day of the week," Robecca chimed in. "Sadly, I can't wear perfume. My steam washes it right off."

"Actually, I was referring to the smell of something gone bad, like, past its expiration date," Toralei corrected Robecca. "Come on, ghouls, don't you know anything? Mummies are rotten."

"Talk about words that could make someone

wilt," Venus mumbled under her breath, clearly shocked by the werecat's comments.

"Toralei, it is my duty as a gargoyle to correct inaccurate information. Therefore, I must tell you: Mummies are not rotten but rather well preserved. To put it simply, Cleo suffers from neither decay nor decomposition," Rochelle stated in a highly matter-of-fact manner.

Toralei squinted and slowly looked the gargoyle up and down, taking in everything from her silver peep-toe shoes to her shimmering rosy locks.

"Oh, I get it now," Toralei hissed. "You dressed up like Ms. Kindergrubber *on purpose*. I've got to say, the scarf's a nice touch."

As Rochelle recoiled in both horror and humiliation, Toralei twitched her perky little ears. It was one of the werecat's most noted idiosyncrasies; she did it to congratulate herself anytime she bested another monster.

"Jeepers! That was weirder than a turtle winning a marathon," Robecca whispered as Toralei glided away with a self-satisfied smile.

"What are you talking about? She always acts like that," Venus shot back with a perplexed expression.

"No, not Toralei! I'm talking about how normal everyone is acting. It's as if they've completely forgotten about the brainwashing episode!"

"You know what, Robecca? You're absolutely right," Venus agreed as she glanced over at the throng of students making their way toward Monster High's main entrance. "Look at them— zombies, werewolves, vampires—they're all totally relaxed, without so much as a lingering suspicion."

"Yes, but to be fair, they don't remember the details like we do. They were in a haze. And without clear, lucid memories, it's much easier for them to move on," Rochelle stated firmly.

"Yeah, but move on to what?" Venus asked solemnly. "What's coming next could be even worse."

CHAPTER two

the unmistakable scent of stewed cabbage and body odor instantly announced the arrival of the trolls. While highly regarded for their pa*troll*ing abilities, the stout creatures with bulbous features were notoriously unhygienic. So unpleasant and gag-inducing was their stench—especially that of their long, greasy locks—that barbershops in town had taken to posting NO TROLLS signs in the windows. And though it reminded the elderly of the days when monsters were ranked by species, no one could blame the barbers. After all, trolls rarely washed

21

their hair more than once a calendar year—twice if they happened to have a date with a non-troll.

"Why no in school?" a chubby troll with a wide variety of moles and dangerously dirty fingernails grunted at Robecca, Rochelle, and Venus in broken English.

"Wow, there really is nothing quite like the scent of troll," Venus mumbled quietly.

"Excuse me, but the bell has not rung. Thus we are not technically required to be inside the school yet," Rochelle politely responded.

Standing directly behind the troll was yet another troll, equally unclean. However, this one was also releasing small showers of saliva with each rattling breath that he drew. Having noted this unfortunate quirk, Venus, Rochelle, and Robecca each took one large step back, silently promising to look into both nose plugs and goggles as soon as possible.

"Hello, ghouls!" called out raven-haired Headless Headmistress Bloodgood as she sauntered up to the students. "Welcome back! How lovely it is not only to see you but to remember you!"

"Does this mean you're no longer suffering from Muddled-Mind Syndrome?" Robecca asked excitedly.

"I'll field that question, non-adult entity," Miss Sue Nami, Monster High's Deputy of Disaster, barked as she barreled toward the group. "While Headmistress Bloodgood has regained a great deal of her memory, she is still suffering from high levels of distractibility. But then again, no one ever said getting struck by lightning was easy."

"They did, however, say lightning doesn't strike twice," Headmistress Bloodgood added, before parting her plump pink lips and breaking into a toothy smile.

"With all due respect, Headmistress, that is factually incorrect," Rochelle clarified. "Lightning can strike, and has struck, the same person twice. And while the odds are low, statistically speaking, it is still possible."

As Robecca and Venus exchanged amused looks over their friend's need to constantly correct people, something splashed across their faces. Miss Sue Nami, a permanently waterlogged monster, had broken into her now-infamous dog shake. Much like a long-haired retriever after a swim, she shook every inch of her robust figure in an effort to stop herself from flooding. So important was the release of water that she did it at least three times an hour, much to the chagrin of those around her.

"Ghouls, what are you still doing out here?

It's the first day of a new semester. You really shouldn't be late," Headmistress Bloodgood advised, dabbing specks of water from her heavily made-up face.

"Unfortunately, we can't go inside until Rochelle's friends Jinafire and Skelita arrive. You see, she promised to show them around on their first day," Robecca explained as Penny and the saliva-spraying troll engaged in a staring contest, which the mechanical penguin quickly won.

"Listen up, non-adult entities. Your information is wrong. Jinafire Long, the dragon from Fanghai, and Skelita Calaveras, the *calaca* from Hexico, arrived at the dormitory late last night, at which time I promptly assigned them to the Chamber of Hairy and Scary."

Upon hearing this news, Venus's nose twitched as her pollens of persuasion rumbled just beneath the surface. Equally annoyed, Robecca released cotton ball–size puffs of steam from her ears. Having sensed her ghoulfriends' extreme aggravation, Rochelle averted her eyes, desperate to avoid their accusatory glares.

"*Je ne comprends pas!* We had a plan! I was supposed to show them around!" Rochelle declared as she nervously tapped her perfectly manicured claws against the wrought-iron gate.

"Rochelle, I do hate to be a pest, but would you mind telling us exactly what they said to you?" Robecca asked as her steam sputtered to a stop.

"When we said *au revoir* at the scareport in Scaris, they told me how happy they were to have someone who could show them the ropes at Monster High."

"And?" Venus interjected in a less-than-friendly tone.

"And seeing as such an activity would logically be handled immediately upon arrival, we've been waiting patiently for them at the gate," Rochelle explained in her typical even-keeled tone.

"Rochelle, I do not wish to be rude. However . . ." started Robecca.

"Robecca, I've got this. I have no problem being rude. Actually, in this instance, I might even enjoy it," Venus said, turning toward Rochelle. "That was not, nor will it ever be, considered a *plan*. Jinafire and Skelita didn't consider it a plan. Robecca and I wouldn't have considered it a plan. And do you know why? Because it's not a plan!" the green-skinned monster huffed as she stomped her boots in frustration.

"Non-adult entities," Miss Sue Nami growled at the ghouls, "in case you've forgotten or cannot read the sign posted to your left, loitering is strictly prohibited."

"This is exactly why I hired Miss Sue Nami. She is absolutely mad about rules!" Headmistress

Bloodgood said as she motioned for the ghouls to follow her into the school.

The sight of Monster High's purple-checked floors and pink coffin-shaped lockers filled Robecca, Rochelle, and Venus with a warm and cozy feeling, one of returning home. Unlike their previous semester at Monster High, now everything was familiar, even the large sign warning that howling, molting fur, bolting limbs, or waking sleeping bats in the hallway was strictly forbidden.

"It's good to be back," Venus said with a smile as she surveyed the corridor brimming with every type of monster imaginable.

"Yes, now let's just hope it stays that way," Rochelle added as she picked up Roux, who was too small to navigate the dense crowd of creatures on her own.

In a sea of monsters chattering and giggling, one flat, emotionless voice quickly garnered the trio's attention. It was, of course, the perennially listless Mr. D'eath.

"I don't mind if you look away while speaking to me. My bony face has been known to incite depression in many a monster, myself included. Hence, the reason I gave all my mirrors to Cleo de Nile; unlike me, she actually takes great pride in looking at herself," the dejected guidance counselor moaned to a young pumpkin head bobbing next to him in the hall.

"Rochelle, are you still planning on resuming your makeover of Mr. D'eath?" Venus asked, all the while watching the dreary guidance counselor shuffle his brown shoes down the corridor.

"Unfortunately, it has come to my attention that

being unhappy is in Monsieur D'eath's bones. And while helping someone become a better version of himself is a wonderful thing, attempting to change who he innately is, is not," Rochelle expounded philosophically as she gently petted Roux's head.

"I think the fact that you even tried to help him says a lot about your character," Venus responded kindly. "And don't forget: Mr. D'eath got a pretty rocking suit out of the whole thing."

"*C'est vrai*, Frankie and Clawdeen did an absolutely *fangtastique* job on the suit," Rochelle agreed.

Venus nodded. "I only wish Mr. D'eath's first time wearing it hadn't been on a date with that dragon who messed with everyone's minds."

"Venus, while I harbor many of the same suspicions you do about Madame Flapper, you must remember that we don't have proof one way or another," Rochelle reprimanded her friend lightly. "We'll just have to wait and see. . . ."

"Wait and see?" Robecca repeated nervously. "That's our plan?"

Rochelle and Venus shrugged.

"That's our plan," echoed Venus.

CHAPTER
three

s the trio walked down the main corridor, a whiff of high-grade oil passed beneath Robecca's petite copper nose. Instantly she was reminded that her mechanical penguin was in need of a little wing maintenance.

"Ghouls, I'm going to pop into Grind 'n' Gears and get Penny a quick oil change," Robecca called out as Rochelle and Venus forged ahead toward the dormitory.

Monster High's auto shop, known as Grind 'n' Gears, was a stainless steel–lined room dedicated to servicing all things mechanical with hydraulic lifts, state-of-the-art oiling apparatuses, and more types of gear grease than salad dressings at a buffet. After bumping into multiple contraptions, knocking over a can of bolts, and screaming "Deary me!" at least three times, Robecca finally summoned a well-oiled mechanical creature with silver-plated limbs and grease-stained coveralls who emerged from the back room.

"What can I do for you?" the piston-powered old man asked while using a nail as a toothpick.

"Mr. Borg, my mechanical penguin Penny's left wing is squeaking, and even though it doesn't bother me in the slightest, I can tell it's driving her absolutely batty. And as you know, batty is not a good thing for a bird."

"Call me Sid. Now take the pipsqueak to oiling station seven while I get my glasses," he replied casually. "This shouldn't take more than a few minutes."

Robecca promptly deposited Penny at oiling station seven, patted her on the head, and began nosing around the auto shop. So many advancements had come to pass while she was disassembled, imbuing her with a great deal of curiosity about all things mechanical.

While fiddling with a sleek metal contraption, Robecca suddenly paused, overwhelmed by a most familiar sensation. She was late. She was absolutely certain of it. Although she hadn't a clue what for. All Robecca knew was that every inch of her copper-plated body was screaming, "You're late!" And so she stormed out of Grind 'n' Gears, having yet again forgotten about Penny.

After successfully navigating the creature-filled corridors, Rochelle and Venus arrived at the creaky, pink spiral staircase that led to the dormitory. And while Rochelle appeared as lithe and slim as any other monster, there was no denying her heavy granite composition as she mounted the stairs.

"*Boo-la-la!* I simply cannot believe this staircase has not been replaced. It must be in violation of at least twenty safety laws, not to mention the law of good taste," Rochelle huffed to Venus, the iron hinges squealing beneath her feet.

"Oh, come on, Rochelle, we both know what this is really about—the screaming sound the stairs make every time you step on them," Venus said with a sly smile.

"You have no idea how difficult it is to be crafted from stone; everything groans and moans beneath me. It's hardly a confidence booster," Rochelle said as she reached the top of the stairs. "*Regardez!* The curtain is even more spooktacular than last semester."

The webbed curtain that hung at the start of the dormitory hall was handcrafted by a group of quarter-size black spiders. And while the drape had always been quite impressive, it was now far more sumptuous and elaborate than ever before.

"It's no wonder the curtain looks so incredible. There are twice as many spiders living in the hall as last semester," Robecca explained as she bounded up the last of the stairs to rejoin her roomies.

"What a relief! I've been concerned I might have let Chewy graze a little too heavily in the hall last semester, if you know what I mean," Venus stated while playfully shaking her head at her pet plant.

"Of course we know what you mean. You very clearly implied that Chewy ate a large portion of the spider population last semester," Rochelle replied earnestly, much to Venus's amusement.

While making their way down the dormitory corridor, they came across many familiar faces, including Rose and Blanche Van Sangre—the gypsy vampire twins with an irksome predilection for sleeping in other people's beds.

"Look, Blanche, it's zose ghouls, ze ones who can never tell us apart," Rose said as she and her sister stopped to glare at Robecca, Rochelle, and Venus in the hall.

"Vat are you, blind? My fangs are viter," Rose declared harshly.

"And my hair is shinier!" Blanche bellowed at an unusually loud decibel.

"Wow, you ghouls are even more peculiar and antisocial than I remember," Venus remarked before moving past the fair-skinned duo with Robecca and Rochelle in tow.

"Get out of our way, we're having a great day, what else can we say? But hip hip hooray!" Sam, Marvin, and James the

pumpkin heads sang as they bobbed through the dormitory, pulling along their leashed pet bullfrogs.

"Maybe pumpkin heads think they live in a musical? It would explain all the singing," Robecca pondered aloud.

"Nah, I think they just enjoy annoying everyone," Venus responded as Rochelle clasped her hands together and hurried down the hall.

"*Boo-jour*, Skelita! Jinafire!" Rochelle screamed joyfully, wrapping her arms around Monster High's newest ghouls.

Dressed in Day of the Dead garb, Skelita had her own style that was an interesting mix of goth and traditional Hexican. Her long black-and-orange hair perfectly complemented her colorful eye makeup and vibrant short skirt. Equally stylish was gold-skinned and long-tailed Jinafire, whose bright green-and-jet-black hair was adorned with an intricate flower headdress.

"These are my friends Robecca and Venus. And these are my other friends Skelita and Jinafire," Rochelle warmly introduced the two sets of ghouls to each other.

"Hey! Welcome to Monster High," Venus offered, before Robecca added, "You guys will absolutely love it here. It really is the cat's pajamas—well, most of the time anyway. . . ."

"And just to be clear, cats do not actually wear pajamas here," Rochelle explained earnestly to Skelita and Jinafire, who both smiled in response.

"*Hola, chicas. ¿Que tal?*" Skelita greeted them.

"*Ni hao,*" Jinafire said while bowing her head slightly. "I am very excited to be here. The other students seem very nice."

"*Sí, sí!* Three-Headed Freddie, Henry Hunchback, Hoodude Voodoo, the pumpkin heads, they're all *estupendos,*" Skelita yammered enthusiastically.

"Actually, I am a little concerned about Hoodude.

He seems rather obsessed with a ghoul named Frankie Stein," Jinafire confessed, before adding, "I do not believe it is *jiankang*, or as you say healthy, to love someone who does not love you back."

Everyone knew that the life-size voodoo doll with buttons for eyes, patchwork skin, and needles sticking out of his body couldn't help but love Frankie; she was, after all, the one who had created him.

"Unrequited love is a serious waste of time," Venus agreed with Jinafire.

"Ugh! Time! It really is such a dreadful word," Robecca asserted as her eyes rapidly scanned the floor. "Frost my firebox! I can't believe I've lost Penny already!"

"You haven't lost her," a soft voice interjected. "You just forgot her at Grind 'n' Gears."

Standing sheepishly behind Robecca with Penny in hand was the incredibly kind one-eyed boy known as Cy Clops.

"Oh, thank you, Cy! As usual you've saved the day," Robecca babbled merrily, throwing her warm copper arm around the boy's shoulder before abruptly pulling away. "Wait, what were you doing at Grind 'n' Gears? You're not mechanical. Or at least you weren't as of last semester. Oh dear, did something happen to you? Were you in an accident? How dreadful! Not that having a mechanical part is the end of the world—"

"No, nothing happened to me. I went over to Grind 'n' Gears to look for you," Cy Clops interrupted quietly. "But I should go now."

And just like that, the boy ran off down the hall.

"*Mi abuela* always says that the shy ones are the best," Skelita stated playfully.

As Robecca smiled coyly, the young Hexican ghoul nudged Jinafire and pointed at her watch.

"I am *very* sorry, but Skelita and I must leave now. We have an appointment with Miss Sue

42

Nami regarding our lockers, which I was very happy to see are pink," Jinafire said, nodding her head politely. "*Zàijiàn*. Bye-bye."

"*Adios*," Skelita added warmly.

Within seconds of the new ghouls' departure, a beautiful spectacle grabbed the attention of Robecca, Rochelle, and Venus. But then again, dressed in a purple pantsuit, sky-high heels, a pearl fanglace, and perfectly styled bloodred hair, Miss Flapper was rather hard to miss.

"Hello, students. Or should I say dormies?" Miss Flapper hissed softly.

"*Pardonnez-moi*, Madame Flapper. What was that you said?" Rochelle asked the delicate dragon.

"After everything that happened last semester, I thought it wise to stay on campus. And as fate would have it, I've been given the room right next door to you ghouls!"

43

CHAPTER four

the start-of-the-term assembly with Head-mistress Bloodgood, Miss Sue Nami, and the rest of the staff was both utterly normal and highly unusual at the same time. It was totally and almost boringly standard in the manner in which classes, social events, and such were addressed. However, it was nothing short of shocking and bizarre that at no time during the assembly did anyone mention the great whisper incident. It really was as if the entire episode had been expunged from Monster High's history.

Following Miss Sue Nami's brusque dismissal

at the end of the assembly, the main hall over-
flowed with ghouls and boys excitedly checking
their iCoffins for their class schedules.

"I've got to say, I commend Headmistress
Bloodgood's rejection of paper schedules. Why kill
trees when you can just as easily send an e-mail?"
Venus mused casually while looking at her bright
pink iCoffin.

"Yes, although I doubt Headmistress Bloodgood is doing it for
environmental reasons. It seems
far more likely she's simply overwhelmed at the idea of keeping
track of so many pieces of paper,

especially in light of her Muddled-Mind Syndrome," Rochelle posited.

"iCoffins, please?" Robecca said as she grabbed
the devices from her friends.

"I still can't believe that before you were dismantled you used a typewriter and a carrier bat for all your correspondence," Venus said, shaking her head in disbelief.

"Actually, Venus, bats have an ability known as echolocation that allows them to use sound waves to identify creatures' and objects' locations. This makes them especially gifted navigators," Rochelle expounded as Venus raised her eyebrows.

"Fine, but you've got to admit, lugging around a heavy typewriter sure does sound like a pain," Venus continued as Robecca pulled up each of the ghouls' schedules on the iCoffins.

"Barking bunnies! We have the same schedule. Well, almost. I have Skultimate Roller Maze instead of Physical Deaducation."

"Great, Phys Dead with Coach Igor," Venus said sarcastically before sighing.

"It might be wise to invest in earplugs. Coach Igor is awfully fond of that whistle," Rochelle cautioned as the first bell of the new semester rang, prompting more than a few of the ceiling bats to flap their wings in protest. With notoriously sensitive ears, the bats had never been too fond of the bells, especially after a long and quiet vacation.

"Come on, ghoulfriends, we don't want to be late for Catacombing: The Art of Digging and Discovery—and not just because tardiness is against school policy. It's also regarded as highly impolite in the Gargoyle Code of Ethics," Rochelle advised the others.

"Is it just me or does Catacombing class sound a lot like playing in the sandbox in elementary school?" Venus joked as the trio started down the corridor.

"It is most definitely just you," Rochelle asserted. "As a matter of fact, there isn't even any sand in the catacombs."

Located deep beneath the halls of Monster

High was a vast collection of stone-lined tunnels known as the catacombs. The series of dimly lit passageways predated the current school structure, although no one could say by how much. All anyone knew for sure was that over the years monsters had taken to hiding relics and other emblems of their time down there. So far underground were the catacombs that an elevator had been installed for efficiency. And though the ornate gold box with carvings of medieval goblins looked as though it dated from the Paleozoic era, it was, in fact, a relatively new addition.

The unusually spacious elevator easily accommodated the many monsters heading down for Catacombing class: Frankie, Hoodude, Draculaura, Cy, Skelita, Jinafire, Cleo, Toralei, and of course Robecca, Rochelle, and Venus.

"It's super voltage being back at school. I always miss everyone so much over vacation," Frankie proclaimed happily to Robecca, Rochelle, and Venus on the ride down.

"Yeah, but you've got to admit that after last semester we all needed a break," Venus responded candidly.

"What do you mean? Because of all the homework Dr. Clamdestine gave us? I guess his reading list was pretty extensive," Frankie conceded.

"This is becoming nuttier than a bowl of almonds and acorns. Why doesn't anybody remember the school being under Miss Flapper's control?" Robecca questioned no one in particular.

"Of course I *remember* it. I just don't think about it. I mean, what's the point? It's over," Frankie countered with a shrug.

"Frankie, I feel it is my duty to point out that at this time, we have no discernible proof that it is either continuing or finished," Rochelle uttered authoritatively.

"Look around, Rochelle. Life is back to normal," Draculaura interjected, before flipping one of her pigtails.

"But that's not to say that any of us has forgotten what you guys did last semester—because we haven't. And as a token of our appreciation, we'd like to invite you ghouls to join the Frightingale Society," Frankie offered with a smile.

Venus, Robecca, and Rochelle squealed in unison, absolutely thrilled by the invitation.

And though the ghouls remained deeply concerned about the school's future, they couldn't help but celebrate the good news. After all, it was quite an honor to be invited to join the Frightingale Society after only one semester at Monster High. Created by the school's founders, the Frightingale Society was an all-ghouls sorority dedicated to community service and fostering lifelong friendships among monsters.

"Oh, *merci boo-coup*! I am so honored to be part of an organization with such an illustrious history," Rochelle prattled graciously to Frankie, just as a long and exaggerated sigh emanated from the royally difficult mouth of Cleo de Nile.

"I thought the Frightingale Society was supposed to be exclusive, as in it *excludes* people," Cleo whined petulantly. "What's next? Are we going to let pets in?"

"Come on, Cleo. Why don't you tell us what

you really think?" Venus retorted sarcastically.

"As far as I'm concerned, the club lost its exclusivity the second it let Cleo in," Toralei huffed, twitching her ears and smirking at the visibly agitated mummy.

Just as the elevator's occupants started to worry that a catfight might break out, the doors slowly parted. Before them was a heart-shaped wrought-iron gate above which hung an antique wooden sign with a hand-carved message: **WELCOME TO THE NORTHERN TUNNELS OF THE CATACOMBS, WHERE HIDDEN FROM LIGHT, IN THE DARK OF NIGHT, YOU JUST MIGHT FIND A MONSTER'S TRUEST FRIGHT.**

Illuminated by wrought-iron sconces, the northern tunnels were lined with smooth gray stones, which fit together seamlessly as though pieces of a puzzle. Intricate carvings of skulls along with life-size portraits of historically important monsters, painted in fluorescent purple, decorated the seemingly endless array of tunnels. Handrails in the form of thick black chains hung ominously across the walls as though imprisoning the many subjects of the paintings.

The faintly lit stone path twisted and turned, passing more than a few digging stations—areas designated for unearthing artifacts—before coming upon the catacombs' sole classroom. The stone-walled room was absolutely brimming with color from the desks and chairs crafted out of brightly painted animal bones, rocks, and twigs. In sharp contrast to the pink, yellow, and red furniture was the black chalkboard on which WELCOME TO CATACOMBING: THE ART OF DIGGING AND DISCOVERY was scrawled messily.

As Robecca entered the classroom, her eyes pricked with tears, which instantly turned to steam. From the second she stepped off the elevator, she'd sensed an undeniable presence, one that she hadn't felt in years—that of her father, Hexicah Steam.

"Robecca? Are you okay?" Venus whispered quietly to her visibly distraught friend.

"I know it was a long time ago, but the catacombs were the last place anyone saw my father," Robecca explained as her eyes continued to steam. "I can't help but think of him and wonder where he is. . . ."

"But I thought your father was a normie?" Venus inquired.

"He was, but he was working on mechanical replacements for normie organs when he disappeared. So who knows? Maybe he's been able to replace his own parts," Robecca said with a sniffle.

"*Ma chérie*, I had no idea your father disappeared in the catacombs," Rochelle expressed sweetly while putting her hand on Robecca's arm. "I'm sure if we explain the situation to Monsieur D'eath, he will happily change us to another class."

"Thanks, but I think it's high time I face my feelings. I've never told anyone this before, but I always thought there was something fishy about my dad's disappearance. Right before it happened he was acting kind of weird—going out at all hours of the night to meet people and talking about how important it was that I lived in a world that treated all monsters equally."

"All monsters equal? I don't think so," Toralei muttered loudly as she pushed past the ghouls and took a seat.

"Ignore her," Cy said quietly as he handed Robecca a tissue.

"Thanks, Cy," Robecca responded softly.

"Anytime," the boy replied shyly, before melting back into the shadows.

As everyone began to sit down, Hoodude grabbed the chair immediately next to Frankie Stein, his consummate crush. And while Cy also wished to sit next to his consummate crush, he didn't want to be nearly as obvious as Hoodude. So instead, the quiet one-eyed boy plopped down in the seat behind Robecca.

"Hello, boys and ghouls," Mr. Mummy announced as he entered the classroom. The always-dapper man was adorned in crisp white gauze, a vest, and a tie.

After placing his leather satchel on his desk, Mr. Mummy smiled fervently at his new crop of students.

"Welcome to Catacombing: The Art of Digging and Discovery. Together we shall explore the vast and seemingly infinite deposits of history hidden throughout the northern tunnels."

Mr. Mummy then began walking through the classroom, occasionally stopping to tap his soft, gauze-covered fingertips against students' desktops.

"As the use of archaeological tools is a messy affair, we have been given two trolls, Trick and Treat, as aides. And before you ask, Trick and Treat are their real names. Apparently, they are quite taken with the normie holiday of Halloween. Now then, they will sweep up, carry heavy artifacts to the elevator, and generally try to maintain some semblance of order down here. But please do not mistake this to mean they work for you, because they don't. Do not ask them to clean your room, because, one, they will have a *troll*iday party in there when you're not home. And, two, it's highly inappropriate. Any questions?"

Excited chatter instantly erupted in the stone-walled classroom. Students were practically exploding with inquiries about everything from the trolls to Mr. Mummy's greatest archaeological find. Yet in the midst of this eagerness and enthusiasm, Robecca sat silently staring at the ground. And it was not because she hadn't any questions—quite the contrary. The young ghoul was absolutely teeming with questions; only they weren't about Catacombing class.

They were about her father.

CHAPTER
five

as the sun slipped behind the mountains, Robecca, Rochelle, and Venus wandered down the main hall. They had finally completed their first day of classes, which included Catacombing, Mad Science, Physical Deaducation, G-ogre-phy, and Home Ick.

From the ceiling came the soft sounds of bats rustling awake. Known as the school's in-house exterminators, they spent their nights prowling for insects and spiders.

"Jeepers creepers! I think that bat just winked at me," Robecca yelped, peering up at the ceiling.

"Maybe he has a crush on you?" Venus joked sarcastically.

"I think it's far more probable that the creature got a bit of dust in his eye and that what Robecca interpreted as a wink was merely a blink. Of course, there is also the possibility that the bat acquired the extremely rare illness known as Winking Bitty Bat Syndrome."

"If you weren't a gargoyle, dedicated to telling the truth, I would never believe you. You've got to admit, Winking Bitty Bat Syndrome sounds pretty silly," Venus said with a giggle.

"It sure does," Robecca agreed.

"I'll have you know that Winking Bitty Bat Syndrome is an entirely real illness. It's named after a bat named Bitty who could not stop winking due to a strange infection in his left eye. Sadly, he spent years being accused of taunting every gargoyle in Scaris before someone finally thought to take him to a doctor," Rochelle recalled solemnly, clearly moved by Bitty Bat's plight.

Upon arriving at the Chamber of Gore and Lore, Robecca, Rochelle, and Venus quickly set about freshening up before dinner. However, in the midst of Rochelle glossing her lips, Venus buffing her leaves, and Robecca greasing her gears, the trio heard something peculiar. It was the familiar sound of footsteps, one after the other, only it was coming from a most unusual place—the ceiling.

"I think someone's up there," Robecca whispered to the others.

"Maybe it's Miss Sue Nami fixing something?" Venus thought aloud.

"With all due respect to Miss Sue Nami, if she were walking across our ceiling, I am rather certain she would crash through," Rochelle pronounced assuredly. "No, it has to be someone lighter, someone with a perfectly logical reason to be walking in the crawl space between the dormitory and the attic."

"Maybe it's a troll sent to rescue a wayward bat?" Robecca posited doubtfully.

"Maybe," Venus mumbled as she followed the footsteps across the room, stopping only when she came to the wall.

A muffled thud reverberated through the plywood and plaster between the rooms, prompting the three ghouls to look at one another curiously.

"Well, whoever it is just jumped into our

64

neighbor's room . . ." Venus trailed off before covering her mouth with her hands in shock.

"Eek! Do you think one of the trolls is a burglar?" Robecca squealed quietly while simultaneously furrowing her brow and frowning.

"Absolutely not, Robecca," Rochelle replied firmly.

"Think about who lives next door," Venus urged.

"Miss Flapper," Robecca mumbled, still unsure of what to make of the situation. "But if it's a troll visiting Miss Flapper, why not use the door? Why sneak in through the ceiling? She is, after all, seen with trolls all the time."

"You make a very good point," Rochelle acknowledged as the sound of an angry yet muffled voice came through the wall.

The trio immediately pressed their ears against the smooth white surface, absolutely desperate to make out what was being said. But alas, it was impossible—the wall was simply too thick. As Rochelle sighed in defeat and Robecca plopped onto a bed, Venus tiptoed over to the window and opened it as quietly as possible.

"You must never come here again! If someone sees you, I'm finished! And I've worked too hard and come too close for this not to succeed!" a stern voice hissed angrily, followed shortly thereafter by the sound of footsteps once again trotting across the ceiling.

After closing the window, Venus, Robecca, and Rochelle huddled together in the far corner of the room.

"Was that Miss Flapper?" Venus whispered to the others. "It sounded like her, only much louder and harsher."

"Pulling pistons! I don't like the way 'I've worked too hard for this not to succeed'

sounded," Robecca muttered nervously.

"I only wish we could have seen who she was talking to," Rochelle said regretfully. "Now then, paragraph 3.9 of the Gargoyle Code of Ethics clearly states that one must share with the authorities any and all information relating to a possible crime. So, with that in mind, I suggest we track down Headmistress Bloodgood and Miss Sue Nami."

"I'm not trying to be a thorn about this, because I know how seriously you take your code of conduct, but I think you're wrong. We don't know who Miss Flapper is working with, so I hardly think it's wise to be talking to anyone at this point," Venus stated confidently.

"In the name of the goat's boat, are you implying Miss Sue Nami or the headmistress could be involved?" Robecca asked with an audible gulp.

"No, I don't think so," Venus said, shaking her

head. "But I just don't think it's smart to talk to them without solid proof. Because if they aren't sure about what we're saying, they could repeat it."

"And that would jeopardize not only our personal safety but the school's," Rochelle agreed.

After waiting patiently for Miss Flapper to exit her room, the ghouls then crept carefully downstairs. However, mere seconds after blending into the crowd of students in the main corridor, Venus spotted the stunningly beautiful dragon speaking with none other than Headmistress Bloodgood.

"Tell me, Rochelle, is there such a thing as Two-Faced Teacher Syndrome?" Venus asked through gritted teeth, her nose twitching as her pollens of persuasion rumbled beneath the surface.

"I can say with absolute certainty that there

is no medically recognized syndrome of that name," Rochelle responded in her formal manner.

"I must say it's a real funky monkey having Miss Flapper living next door to us. Talk about heebie-jeebie central," Robecca mumbled. "Oh, just thinking about it makes me steam up."

"*S'il ghoul plaît*, Robecca, you must calm down or you'll be damp and frizzy before we even reach the Creepateria," Rochelle advised her friend as Miss Flapper, now dressed in a floor-length violet gown, ambled away from the headmistress.

"Come on, ghouls, let's do a little investigating," Venus said as she approached Headmistress Bloodgood.

"Well, if it isn't three of my favorite students—tied with your classmates, of course. As you know, a headmistress cannot play favorites. Now then, if this is about a schedule change, you're going to have to speak with Mr. D'eath. Last I heard he

was having a picnic by himself in the middle of the Casketball court.

Speaking of which, the court is in desperate need of a wax. It's getting so that I can barely see my own reflection in it. Anyway, I really must be going, but thank you so much for bringing the terrible state of the Casketball court to my attention."

"Um, actually, we didn't. We haven't even had a chance to say anything yet," Venus stated awkwardly.

"Really?" Headmistress Bloodgood responded with a most puzzled expression. "My apologies, ghouls. Now then, what can I do for you?"

"It's about the incident last semester. Have you heard anything else?" Venus inquired.

"Of course, the incident," Headmistress Bloodgood said

with a knowing nod. "You mean when Hoodude asked Frankie to marry him? He really can be such a silly boy."

"Good golly, Headmistress, have you forgotten about the whisper incident already?" Robecca wondered aloud.

"Oh, you're talking about *that*. Really, ghouls, you mustn't dwell on the past. That's all behind us now," Headmistress Bloodgood reassured the students. "You see, Miss Sue Nami and I have come to realize that the whisper arrived at Monster High by *accident*. Poor Miss Flapper hadn't a clue she was even doing it. Now then, I insist you put all this nonsense out of your minds," she instructed the students forcefully before joining Sam, Marvin, and James the pumpkin heads as they bobbed down the hall singing, "*We are back at school, among the ghouls, we only hope they don't think us fools!*"

"I must say, they are very musical, very *yinyue* indeed," Jinafire assessed as she walked up to the three ghouls, paused to subtly bow, and then smiled.

"*Sí, sí!* We can even hear them singing through the dorm walls," Skelita added as she joined the group.

"Ghouls, I am so happy to have run into you," said Rochelle. "How are you finding everything? Do you have any safety issues? The bats? The creaky staircase in the dormitory? I am here to help allay any and all of your concerns."

"Ah, *gracias*, Rochelle. But you really don't need to worry about us, we're fine," Skelita replied warmly.

"Yes, it is true, we are very happy here, especially because of Miss Flapper. She is a wonderful woman," Jinafire offered.

"*Sí, sí! Me gusta* Miss Flapper," Skelita seconded, before the two waved good-bye and continued down the hall.

"It looks like Miss Flapper found some new fans," Robecca muttered quietly.

"Fans?" Venus replied suspiciously. "More like targets."

CHAPTER
Six

ollowing a most delightful dinner of Zombie Stew, a savory soup cooked *very* slowly, Robecca, Rochelle, and Venus headed to the Arts and Bats room for their very first Frightingale Society meeting. As this was the school's most popular all-ghouls club, they were understandably a bit nervous and apprehensive about what to expect. Both Rochelle and Robecca fiddled nervously with their accessories, while Venus fussed over her long pink-and-green-striped hair.

Upon arriving at the room with craft supplies

and bats, the trio found it a great deal more sophisticated than usual, with large bouquets of pink roses, plaid tablecloths, and a wide variety of mouthwatering desserts. Even the walls were decorated with posters of successful ghouls, like sea creature Gillary Clinton, werecat Feral Streak, centaur Tina Hay, and so many more.

"I must say this really is the bee's knees! Can you believe we're actually members of such a prestigious club?" Robecca gushed as Venus and Rochelle sampled the chocolate chip cookies, coconut cake, and éclairs.

"After a stressful day, this is just what I needed," Venus said as she shoved an enormous hunk of cake into her mouth.

"Jeez, Venus, you look like Chewy with a bracelet the way you're going after that coconut cake," Robecca teased lightheartedly.

"It's most ironic that a plant named Chewy

hasn't a clue how to chew," Rochelle asserted, before crying out, "What if he chokes? None of us knows how to administer the Heimlich maneuver to a plant!"

"Relax. If Chewy hasn't choked yet on a diet of jewelry, matchbooks, and pebbles, I think he's in the clear," Venus reassured Rochelle as Frankie motioned for everyone to take a seat.

Draculaura joined Frankie at the front of the Arts and Bats room, both sporting superchic ensembles. Frankie wore a blue plaid skirt with a matching sweater, while Draculaura opted for a pink dress with white lace trim and knee-high boots.

"Are you guys okay? You're both trembling," Venus whispered to Rochelle and Robecca.

"Shhh, we're just excited," Robecca responded, determined not to miss a single word that Frankie and Draculaura uttered.

"As copresidents of the Frightingale Society, Draculaura and I would like to welcome you to another great semester at Monster High," Frankie announced while fidgeting with one of her silver neck bolts.

"We are, as most of you know, a sorority dedicated to helping others and making lifelong ghoulfriends," Draculaura added. "And so, with this in mind, I am making Project Scare and Care the first order of business. For those of you who don't remember, this is one of our community-service programs."

"Now don't freak out; we're not talking about cleaning bathrooms or painting walls," said Frankie with a smile.

"Thank Ra!" Cleo interjected. "I spend a lot of time and money keeping my nails finely manicured."

"Project Scare and Care asks monsters to share

one of their skills with the school," Draculaura continued. "For example, I'm going to team up with Ms. Kindergrubber to offer vegetarian cooking lessons for anyone looking to go meat-free."

"And I'm partnering up with Clawdeen to help ghouls design and sew their own voltage outfits," Frankie said cheerfully. "Does anyone have any ideas about what they'd like to do?"

After a few seconds of hushed whispers, a hand went up *very slowly* at the back of the room. It was Ghoulia Yelps, who, as usual, was mumbling in Zombese.

"The school's smartest ghoul offering free tutoring? That's amazing," Frankie translated for those unable to understand Ghoulia's native tongue.

"Hey, mates, I'm thinking about doing something for the environment, maybe starting a recycling program," Lagoona offered casually.

"How about starting a compost pile with me instead?" Venus replied enthusiastically.

"Absolutely! I'm in," Lagoona agreed. "I always say we need to cut down on our trash, and a compost pile is the perfect way to do it."

"You *would* say that," Toralei scoffed. "Well, I guess if I have to do something, I'll allow one of the school's starving artists to draw my *purrfect* face."

Frankie and Draculaura briefly exchanged amused looks before regaining their composure.

"Actually, Toralei, we were hoping you might plan the Hex Factor Talon Show. It's the new and improved version of the Talon Show, and organizing it will require someone with a . . ." Frankie paused, desperately racking her mind for a polite way to say "bossy."

"Strong personality," Draculaura finished.

"Excuse me?" Cleo cried as she jumped to her feet. "As one of the school's most *talented* ghouls, don't you think *I* should be in charge of the Hex Factor Talon Show? Plus, I'm royalty, so judging people comes naturally to me."

"Hold on a second," Draculaura said, before whispering in Frankie's ear for a moment.

"After discussing the possibilities, we have come to realize that the best solution is for you ghouls to cochair the Hex Factor Talon Show. That way both of you get to participate, plus maybe it will help you ghouls improve your friendship," Frankie announced apprehensively.

"You mean you want *me* to partner with *her*?" Toralei snapped, glaring at Cleo. "A were-cat working with a second-rate royal? I don't think so."

"Second in line to the throne but *never* second-rate. Not that I would expect a lowly *alley cat* like yourself to understand such a thing," Cleo shot back angrily.

As the school's biggest divas exchanged grimaces, Frankie and Draculaura continued on with the meeting. Rochelle promptly offered to tutor trolls in English and hygiene, while Robecca agreed to teach Skultimate Roller Maze to the athletically challenged.

By the time the gathering had finished, Robecca, Rochelle, and Venus were so tired, they could think of nothing they wanted to do more than climb into bed and pull the covers over their heads.

"Penny better not be a bed hog tonight," Robecca muttered as she entered the Chamber of Gore and Lore.

"That's one upside to having a pet plant; he doesn't share the bed," Venus said, stifling a yawn.

"No, but he does eat jewelry and occasionally even fingers," Robecca pointed out.

"It's not Chewy's fault. He can't see very

well. He has no choice but to nibble first and ask questions later," Venus grumbled while pulling off her pink boots.

First Venus, then Robecca, and finally Rochelle flopped onto their beds and sighed loudly. But then the trio of ghouls heard two *more* sighs. Alarmed by the sounds, Rochelle jumped out of bed to inspect the room. She very quickly discovered one of the Van Sangre sisters (though she couldn't tell which) sleeping under her bed.

"*Quelle horreur!* What are you doing under here?" Rochelle gasped.

"Taking a nap. Vat are you doing vaking me up?" Blanche muttered in response.

"No way, you two," Venus snapped, having just discovered Rose under her bed. "Get out of here!"

"Vhy must you guys be so difficult? Ve are just a couple of gypsy vampires looking for a place to rest," Rose whined.

83

"You do realize that the school has provided an appropriate place for you to sleep. It's called your room," Rochelle explained.

"Gypsy vampires do not like to stay put," Rose said as she and Blanche climbed out from under the beds.

Both dressed in polka-dot nightdresses and long velvet robes, the two slowly began stretching as if to wake themselves up.

"Ghouls, calisthenics class is going to have to wait. We're going to bed," Venus said as her vines tightened around her arms.

"I zink you owe us an apology," Blanche demanded seriously.

"For what?" Venus asked, utterly apoplectic.

"Zat plant ate my ring," Rose snapped. "And zat one ripped Blanche's stockings while jumping at her feet," she continued, pointing to Roux. "But the vorst vas the metal bird staring at us. . . . Zat zing is plain creepy!"

The three ghoulfriends instantly burst out laughing, amazed by how well the Van Sangre sisters already knew their pets. Believing that Robecca, Rochelle, and Venus were laughing at them, Blanche and Rose turned up their noses and stormed angrily out of the room.

The sun had barely crested over the scattering of clouds when Robecca flung back her comforter, grabbed Penny, and dashed out of her dorm room without so much as a word to her sleeping roommates.

"I'm late! I'm late! Why am I always so late?" Robecca mumbled to herself as she stormed down the dormitory hall, taking out the silky spider curtain in the process.

It wasn't until the time-challenged ghoul found the Creepateria door locked that it occurred to her that she might not be late, but really, really early instead.

"Oh, Penny! I was so sure I was late; I didn't even think to see if Rochelle and Venus were still in the room. Why is it that time is never on my side?"

Later that morning Rochelle and Venus sat in the Libury researching the school's floor plan in an attempt to see how Miss Flapper's visitor might have accessed the crawl space between the attic and the dormitory's ceiling. With both of their heads buried in blueprints, they heard a familiar screeching sound reverberate throughout the quiet, dust-filled room.

"Looking for us?" Venus asked, flinging her pink-and-green hair over her shoulder.

"*Boo-la-la*, Robecca! Where have you been? It's most disconcerting to start the day with a missing roommate," Rochelle huffed, "especially in light of our new neighbor."

"Relax, Rochelle," said Venus. "Robecca disappearing is as normal as the sun rising in the east and setting in the west. To be honest, if she didn't disappear occasionally, I'd start to worry."

"Ghouls! We haven't time for this," Robecca muttered nervously. "Oh, just thinking about what I saw makes me want to steam clean my memory!"

"What did you see? Was it Miss Flapper? Did you find out who came to see her?" Venus asked animatedly.

"Or something worse? Has she brought a new plague to Monster High? *S'il ghoul plaît*! I can't take it! You must tell us!" Rochelle pleaded.

"Okay," Robecca said as she slowly sat down at the table and began pulling twigs from her hair.

"Seriously, what happened? It looks like you were attacked by an elm tree or something," Venus said as she inspected Robecca closely.

"Actually, I kind of was. . . ."

"This is starting to sound *très* bizarre," Rochelle squawked anxiously.

"After I realized that I hadn't overslept and had actually woken up really early, I decided to go ahead and post flyers for my Skultimate Roller Maze lessons," Robecca stated apprehensively. "Only, while Penny and I were jetting around campus . . . I saw . . ."

"Saw what?" Venus screeched impatiently.

"A white cat! I was so terrified that I slammed into a tree! And, even worse, I lost Penny in the crash! Do you think the white cat has done something to her?"

"No, of course not. Knowing Penny, she probably scared the cat off with her stink eye," Venus tried to reassure Robecca, albeit not very convincingly.

"It's a sign. Whatever Miss Flapper is planning to do is going to be very, very bad," Robecca babbled, rife with fear.

"A white cat is not good . . . not good at all," Venus seconded as she pulled at her vines. "Is it me or is it starting to feel like a greenhouse in here?"

"It's you," Rochelle replied curtly as she shook her head and sighed, clearly dismayed by the conversation. "White cats are no more a threat to us than black cats are to normies. This is nothing more than a silly monster superstition—"

"But I've heard stories," Venus interrupted.

"About them being bad omens? Oh, what

nonsense! I thought you ghouls were smarter than this," the levelheaded gargoyle snapped, packing up her book bag.

"You've got to admit, Rochelle, in light of what we just heard, it could mean something," Robecca said softly, almost reticently.

"It means you two are more susceptible to silly stories than I previously thought. Now that is not to say that we aren't in danger; we very well might be, but it has nothing to do with a white cat," Rochelle replied, before looking directly at Robecca. "And please comb your hair before class. It looks like a forest, there are so many twigs in there!"

"Where are you going?" Venus called out as Rochelle made her way toward the door.

"I have my first session with Trick and Treat this morning."

"The trolls from Catacombing class?" Robecca asked.

"Yes, they were the first ones to sign up. They are clearly very eager to improve their English and learn about hygiene," Rochelle explained as she waved good-bye.

Rochelle chose the Study Howl for her first troll-tutoring session for two very good reasons: one, it was quiet; and two, there wasn't any food available. Having previously seen trolls eat, she knew it was wise to avoid experiencing it up close. Unfortunately, she hadn't realized that, even without food, seeing trolls up close was a rather memorable occurrence.

Seated two feet away from the trolls' greasy, grimy, and gritty faces, Rochelle was able to see a myriad of small bumps and pimples she had not noticed before. And while her syllabus currently did not contain a section on dermatology, she recognized the need to amend it.

"After squeezing a pea-size portion of antibacterial soap into your hand . . ." Rochelle trailed off, distracted by the sight of Trick using her pen as a toothbrush. "Trick, putting other monsters' belongings in your mouth without their permission is considered *très* rude."

"Rude!" Treat repeated, before wiping his nose on Rochelle's yellow Scaremès scarf.

"You may consider that an early birthday present," Rochelle said as she recoiled at the sound of Treat's mucus flowing into the fine silk fabric. "Now then, after applying a pea-size quantity of antibacterial soap . . ."

"Pea-size! Pea-size!" Trick chanted.

"Yes," Rochelle said through gritted teeth while

tapping her claws impatiently on the tabletop. "You then place your hands under the water . . ."

"Under table! Under table!" Treat grunted and then lowered himself beneath the table.

"No, Treat! No! I said under the *water*, as in you place your soapy hands under the *water*! Not under the *table*!" Rochelle moaned with frustration as she continued to click her claws harshly against the desktop.

"Hey, what'd that table ever do to you?" a smooth voice called out to Rochelle.

Instantly pumped with adrenaline, having recognized the voice as Deuce's, Rochelle quickly looked away with embarrassment.

"*Zut!* Sometimes I forget how strong I am," Rochelle lamented as she looked down at the cracked table.

"Hey, Trick. Hey, Treat," Deuce said to the trolls while offering a friendly head nod.

Both Trick and Treat immediately calmed down, clearly intimidated by Deuce—and with good reason. The story of Deuce accidentally turning one of their colleagues to stone the previous semester had quickly spread through the troll community.

"I've got to say, I'm a little surprised to see you hanging out with trolls. Did you have a fight with Robecca and Venus?" Deuce asked while fiddling with his snake-filled Mohawk.

"No, of course not. They're my best ghoulfriends. As part of my Frightingale duties, I've volunteered to tutor trolls in hygiene and English. However, getting them to listen to me is harder than getting Robecca to class on time."

"Really? They always seem to listen to me. I can help you out if you'd like," Deuce proposed generously.

"You would do that for me?" Rochelle blathered as she blushed.

"After what you did for the school last semester? Of course!"

"You're the first monster to even bring that up. It's like everyone else has forgotten. They're not even worried that it might happen again," Rochelle said while shaking her head, clearly confused by her classmates' lack of concern.

"It's not that everyone has forgotten. It's that when we look around, we don't see any reason for concern. Everything looks pretty normal. And as we all know, there's no use worrying about something that might not even happen," Deuce explained, breaking into a smile.

"That's easy for you to say; you're not a gargoyle."

CHAPTER
seven

the scent of cheese casketdillas wafted through the Creepateria as students swapped tales about the start of school, discussing everything from their teachers' clothes to the new captain of the Skultimate Roller Maze team. Positioned conspicuously among the young monsters were the lunch monitors, Mr. D'eath and Miss Sue Nami. Seated in bone-cold silence, Mr. D'eath mentally reviewed his regret list while Miss Sue Nami considered how best to handle the increasing amount of lip she was receiving from the trolls.

Two tables away, engrossed in a most serious conversation about cleaning up the environment, were Lagoona and Venus.

"I just don't get it, mate. We only have one planet. Why are we trashing it? And I mean that literally: Why are we stashing trash inside mountains?" Lagoona asked as she lifted her cheese casketdilla to her mouth.

"Don't even get me started on landfills; just the thought of them makes my pollen go crazy! How could anyone think stuffing a mountain with trash is a good idea? How is that a viable long-term solution to our waste problem? I mean, is anyone in graverment even paying attention?" Venus asked with palpable frustration.

"Sometimes it doesn't feel like it, but there must be other monsters concerned about the oceans and forests and—"

"Excuse me, ghouls," a velvety voice interrupted.

Standing before Lagoona and Venus, dressed in a leopard-print jumpsuit and a bedazzled red belt, was none other than Toralei Stripe. As the werecat rarely graced her classmates with her presence in the Creepateria, the two environmentalists were more than a little taken aback.

"I hate to bother you ghouls while you're chowing, but I was wondering if you could sign my petition. It's super important," Toralei said as she batted her long feline eyelashes.

"You started a petition? For what? To put milk in the drinking fountains?" Venus said with a giggle.

"A cat joke? How lame. But then again, what else should I expect from a lowly house plant?" Toralei responded harshly.

"Always such a pleasure," Venus mumbled sarcastically to herself.

"So what's the petition about, mate?" Lagoona asked curiously.

"There are these two super weird ghouls trying to turn Monster High's back field into a trash dump. It's just not right, so I'm going to stop them," Toralei explained.

"A trash dump? Don't you mean a compost pile?" Lagoona inquired with a perplexed expression.

"Same thing. So can I get your signature or what?" Toralei demanded with a self-satisfied smirk.

"Toralei, we're trying to save the planet by recycling things that are biodegradable. How could you possibly have a problem with that? Don't you want the planet to be clean for your children and grandchildren?" Venus expounded passionately.

"Listen up, ghouls, it's super simple. I don't like to be surrounded by trash," Toralei said cuttingly, twitching her ears, before sashaying away from the table.

"I just don't get her," Venus stated honestly. "She's such a mully."

"A what?" Lagoona asked as she cocked her head to the side.

"A monster plus a bully equals a mully," Venus enlightened Lagoona, much to the sea creature's amusement.

"Did you just make that up?" Lagoona asked, breaking into a smile.

"Of course. I'm more than just an environmentalist; I'm also a wordsmith," Venus proclaimed as Lagoona stood up. "Hey, where are you going?"

"I'm meeting Gil at the pool. I'll catch you later, mate," she said, before offering Venus a hang-ten sign and walking away.

Fortunately for Venus, she wasn't alone for long.

"Eating alone in the Creepateria? Deary me! Whatever is the matter?" Robecca asked as she, Skelita, and Rochelle approached the table.

"Nothing. I'm just nursing my wounds after a visit from Toralei. She's trying to close down the compost pile; she's started a petition and everything."

"*Que nada, chica*. Toralei doesn't have enough friends to get the required number of signatures. I might be new, but even I can see that," Skelita said as she sat down next to Robecca.

"Skelita, I couldn't help but notice your incredible crocheted shrug. Is that from Hexico?" Rochelle asked, admiring the delicate material.

"It's beautiful, isn't it?" Skelita agreed while looking at her own shrug. "Senorita Flapper loaned it to me. She's such a wonderful dragon. And have you seen her wardrobe? It's all couture. The ghouls in Hexico would die if they saw it!"

"She's definitely stylish, I'll give her that," Venus said through gritted teeth.

"And so helpful as well. She's becoming like a *hermana mayor*, a big sister, to Jinafire and me."

"A big sister? Wow, she's clearly won you over. And in such a short amount of time too," Venus assessed while shooting Robecca and Rochelle suspicious looks.

"I know. Usually it takes me ages to feel close to someone, but with Senorita Flapper, it's happened so quickly for both Jinafire and me."

"Yeah, it's almost like she's cast a spell on you," Venus said before Rochelle and Robecca broke in with forced laughter.

"She's kidding! Obviously," Robecca babbled uncomfortably to the *calaca*.

"I know," Skelita said with a smile. "I think more than anything the friendship has developed because Senorita Flapper has really taken the time to get to know me. Like last night, she stayed up super late talking to Jinafire and me about our families. She even managed to make me feel better about spending Day of the Dad away from my father," Skelita said sincerely.

"I've never been to a Hexican Day of the Dad celebration, but I imagine it's *fangtastique*," Rochelle interjected.

"Oh yes, we have a huge fiesta, complete with a mariachi band and everything," Skelita explained as small bursts of steam exited Robecca's eyes.

"Are you okay, *ma chérie*?" Rochelle inquired compassionately.

"I'm sorry, I don't know what's gotten into me lately. Ever since that first day in the catacombs, I can't stop thinking about my father. He was such a swell guy. I think you ghouls would really like him. And of course he'd like you too!"

Rochelle and Venus grabbed hold of Robecca's copper hands and squeezed tightly, helping her weather the emotional storm.

Just then a high-pitched shriek ripped through the Creepateria, instantly alarming all within earshot.

Eyes darted frenetically around the room, searching for the origin of the scream, until Frankie Stein slowly rose from her chair. The mint-green ghoul's delicate hands were clasped over her mouth as the students followed her gaze to the ceiling, where an albino bat quietly flapped its wings. Stark white and approximately the size of a house cat, the creature appeared rather angelic, at least to the unmonstrous eye. For just as monsters viewed white cats as omens of bad, terrible, horrendous luck, white bats were also bad signs.

Gasps, whispers, and cries tore through the room as ghouls and boys alike fretted that they might never make it out of the Creepateria alive.

"What's coming? What terrible thing is going to happen to us?" Frankie babbled as Robecca and Venus exchanged a nervous look. Although both loathed admitting it to the ever-logical Rochelle, they too believed that white cats and bats were omens of bad luck.

"Absolutely nothing is going to happen! *Rien!* Or if something does happen, it will have nothing to do with a bat!" Rochelle stated firmly, having stood up on her chair to make sure everyone could hear her. "There is unquestionably no truth to this legend of white cats and bats bringing bad luck. It's all just superstitious nonsense!"

Voices of dissent quickly sprang up all over the Creepateria, much to Rochelle's surprise.

"What does she know? She's just a gargoyle."

"Poor kid, she has her head stuck so far in the gravel, she doesn't even know what's happening."

"Bad luck will probably strike her first, then her pet griffin."

"What a stone head!"

"*S'il ghoul plaît*, think about this logically," Rochelle pleaded from atop her perch, which was now creaking loudly under her weight.

"Rochelle? I think you need to step down," Venus instructed her friend as Skelita slipped away, hiding behind a nearby garbage can.

"But I must try to reason with our classmates. It's my duty as a gargoyle," Rochelle proclaimed seriously.

"Okay, but we're pretty sure the chair's going to collapse any second now," Robecca interjected, instantly prompting Rochelle to step down.

"Now that I think about it, I can reason just as well from down here as from up there," Rochelle said as she surveyed the many frightened faces in the crowd.

"Non-adult entities," Miss Sue Nami roared as she jumped up from the lunch monitors' table. "Step to the back of the Creepateria and wait for the appropriate authorities to arrive and handle the intruder."

"Appropriate authorities? Intruder?" Rochelle repeated in shock. "It's a bat! There are a thousand of them living in the corridors. The only difference is this one's white. Can't you see? It's discrimination, plain and simple."

But alas no one listened to Rochelle; they merely continued to whisper, whimper, and whine about the loathsome bat.

"That's it! I'm going to handle this situation myself," Rochelle proclaimed to Robecca and Venus.

"What in the name of the flea's sneeze are you going to do?" Robecca asked Rochelle as small traces of steam exited her ears.

"I am going to humanely capture the creature, using one of my trusted accessories," Rochelle said as she pulled a new Scaremès scarf from her bag. "Now I just need to find a ladder."

However, as Rochelle started toward the supply cupboard, the Creepateria doors flew open, smashing thunderously against the wall.

"Has anyone seen a white bat?" Henry Hunchback shrieked hysterically.

Covered head to toe in a thick white residue, similar to the consistency of maple syrup, Henry looked as though he'd been dunked in paint. After momentarily pausing to take in the boy's odd appearance, the students silently pointed to the bat flapping quietly in the corner.

"Non-adult entity, you have a lot of explaining to do. As you can imagine, the arrival of a white bat has caused a great deal of anxiety in the students," Miss Sue Nami bellowed, before beginning an epic shake all over Henry. But seeing as he was covered head to toe in white goo, he hardly minded.

"It all started when I was in Mad Science class. I wasn't really paying attention when Mr. Hack explained the experiment. Instead, I was thinking about what Coach Igor had said about improving my Casketball game—"

"This explanation is taking too long. Get to the point, or you will have detention in the dungeon, or as I call it the no-fungeon," Miss Sue Nami interrupted.

"I messed up the experiment, so I had to stay in at lunch to redo it. Only, I messed it up again, and this time it exploded all over me and the bat!"

"Okay, non-adult entity, but that still doesn't explain how the bat got in here."

"I thought it would be funny to leave the little guy in my dorm room as a joke, to mess with my roommate, Cy. But as you can see, he got away from me. . . ."

As the Creepateria erupted in laughter, Robecca, Venus, and Rochelle looked at one another and smiled.

"Honestly, ghouls, you mustn't believe in superstition, only cold, hard facts," Rochelle lectured her friends.

"Oh? You mean like the fact that Miss Flapper is planning something with someone, and we still don't have a clue about any of it?" Venus quipped.

"Yes, exactly," Rochelle said, clearly deflated by Venus's reminder.

CHAPTER eight

Venus awoke to a gray and overcast sky devoid of even the faintest hint of blue. The absence of the sun always left the ghoul feeling rather gloomy; she was a plant, after all. Pushing back her mummy-gauze and werewolf-fur sheets, the green ghoul crept out of bed, grabbed the watering can, and gave Chewy his morning shower. As the droplets dribbled down her pet plant's leaves, Venus turned her gaze toward the fledgling compost pile.

In the nine hours since Venus had last looked out her dormitory window, the small recycling area for biodegradable substances had been vandalized. A slew of hand-painted signs proclaiming there's no room for trash at monster high now surrounded the perimeter of the compost pile. Her physical reaction was instantaneous: Her temperature rose, her nose twitched, and her eyes watered. Venus's anger grew exponentially as she thought of Toralei, 100 percent certain the werecat was responsible for the defacement.

Seething with rage, Venus could no longer control herself or her nose. The young ghoul exploded, quite literally, all over the glass. So loud and boisterous was the sneeze that it jolted both Rochelle and Robecca awake.

"*C'est très interessant.* It looks like a piece of modern art," Rochelle mused as she gazed at the large orange splotches of pollen on the glass.

"Jeez Louise, that doesn't speak very highly of modern art, does it?"

"Did you see what Toralei did to the compost pile? I have half a mind to tell Frankie and Draculaura at the next Frightingale Society meeting! I mean seriously, what is wrong with her? Why is she such a mully?" Venus raged, slamming her well-manicured feet against the floor.

"I loathe correcting you at a moment like this, but as you know, I have a duty. *Mully* is not a real word, and the simple act of saying it cannot make it one," Rochelle clarified in a dry, almost academic tone.

Venus's eyes suddenly pricked with water as her nose once again began to twitch.

"Rochelle, maybe now isn't the best time to dissect the legitimacy of Venus's vocabulary," Robecca advised as she stepped out of the line of fire.

"But paragraph 11.3 of the Gargoyle Code of Ethics explicitly states that one must never allow poor timing to interfere with the truth."

And with that, Venus released another sneeze, albeit smaller, all over Rochelle. Dusted in orange powder, the granite ghoul immediately broke into the most peculiar grin.

"*Merci boo-coup*, Venus! You're absolutely right: Toralei is a mully. And as a matter of fact, I plan on announcing just that at our next Frightingale Society meeting," Rochelle yammered, her eyes glazed over.

"Oh brother, this is not good," Robecca said as she and Penny shook their heads judgmentally at Venus.

An hour later, looking as though she had engaged in an epic fake-tanning session, Rochelle made her way toward the elevator to the catacombs. While silently smarting over her orange glow, she felt something pull at her sweater, then her arm, then her leg, until small greasy hands were literally pulling her every which way. Surrounded by a mass of foul-smelling, greasy-haired, saliva-spewing trolls, Rochelle sighed loudly. Today just wasn't her day.

"We no like homework," one of the trolls grunted angrily in her face.

"No homework! You do it! We no do it!" another troll screamed while punching his fist dramatically in the air.

"*S'il ghoul plaît*, you must understand that homework is an essential part of learning, as it reinforces the ideas taught in class," Rochelle explained warily as two of the trolls began wagging their crusty fingers in her face.

"Hey! Knock it off, trolls! That's no way to treat

a ghoul," Deuce harshly reprimanded the stout beasts.

"Sorry, Dos," the trolls muttered before lowering their heads and dispersing.

So romantic and chivalrous was the moment that Rochelle half expected Deuce to be on a horse with the sun setting behind him.

"Deuce! *Merci boo-coup!* That was so kind of you," Rochelle gushed. "I had no idea homework would incite such hostility in the trolls."

"I think they just like to be angry. Plus, they all have Napoleon complexes about their height," Deuce teased as Cleo walked up behind them.

"I'm absolutely furious! I just checked my iCoffin, and you won't believe what that wicked werecat said!" Cleo raged, pulling at her gold arm bandages in frustration.

The ill-tempered mummy then lightly kicked a nearby locker with her gold boot. It was at this exact moment that Cleo happened to glance up and see Toralei sashaying straight toward her.

"The Hex Factor is in less than three weeks, and in case you've forgotten, we're cochairs, as in equal partners. So stop trying to boss me around," Cleo seethed at Toralei.

"Equal partners? That's rich. You told me to curtsy to you," Toralei shot back.

"Only after you implied that werecats were more important than royal mummies in your creature hierarchy!"

"I don't care what you say. We're doing *my* ideas for the Hex Factor because they're better. So do me a favor and climb back into whatever tomb you came from!"

"No way, *cat lady*! We're either meeting in the middle, as in a compromise, or we're not doing anything at all!" Cleo screeched.

"*Cat lady*? I'd be careful if I were you. I just sharpened my claws," Toralei said pointedly as she twitched her ears.

"You're threatening me? How feral."

"Toralei, why don't you take the elevator to the catacombs first? I think it's best you two travel separately," Deuce said calmly while pulling Cleo away from her rival.

Despite the wide array of hissing and groaning, Toralei and Cleo consented to being separated, forgoing the impending mummy-versus-werecat smack-down.

Catacombing class began as it always did: with a lecture on the importance of wearing safety goggles and gloves while digging. And though neither Mr. Mummy nor Rochelle ever told anyone, this daily safety reminder had been her idea. She found that teenage monsters were too self-obsessed to remember much of anything outside themselves and, therefore, required frequent prompting.

"Remember, boys and ghouls, it's always best to investigate with a steady hand and an open mind," Mr. Mummy said as he motioned for the students to head into the tunnels and begin excavating.

"Okay, ghouls, grab your tools. Let's get digging," Robecca instructed while putting on her gloves and safety goggles.

"Tools? What do you think these are?" Rochelle said as she lifted up her well-manicured claws. "Even Trick and Treat think they're better than any of the tools in here."

"Trick and Treat," Robecca repeated as she glanced over at the sour-faced trolls. "I would never say this in front of Penny, but there's something about trolls that reminds me of her. I just can't put my finger on it."

"As you know, my code of conduct requires that I answer your question honestly. It's Penny's disagreeable facial expressions. She, like the trolls, always looks very unhappy, *très grognon*."

"Abort, abort," Venus whispered to Rochelle, having noted small wisps of steam descending from Robecca's nostrils.

"You think Penny looks unhappy? Like she has a permanent bee in her bonnet?" Robecca inquired emotionally.

"Yes, of course she looks unhappy. That's why Venus calls her Pouty Penny," Rochelle replied candidly—perhaps too candidly.

"Seriously, Rochelle? Was that last tidbit really necessary?" Venus huffed.

"Do you think it's me? Do you think I'm the

reason Penny is so unhappy?" Robecca wondered aloud while suffering from a dreadful combination of guilt and self-doubt.

"Absolutely not. It's just who she is, sort of like how Rochelle's a gargoyle who cannot help but tell the truth even when it's really inappropriate and super annoying," Venus said, eyeing her stone-bodied friend.

"Ghouls? Perhaps you didn't realize it, but this is Catacombing class, not Chatting class. And in case you haven't noticed, all your classmates have already begun digging," Mr. Mummy said with both hands firmly attached to the lapels of his blue sweater-vest.

"Sorry, Mr. Mummy. We'll get straight to digging," Robecca mumbled as she started for the closest tunnel.

"I suspect most of the stations in there have already been taken. Why don't you try another tunnel instead?" Mr. Mummy said, pointing toward one on the far side of the classroom.

The narrow, dimly lit passageway was rather austere, lacking both the skull carvings and the life-size portraits found elsewhere in the catacombs. A few wrought-iron sconces and the chain handrail were the only embellishments found in the tunnel. Located directly in the center of a hairpin turn was the lone digging station, and from the looks of it, it had not been in use for quite some time.

After the turn, the tunnel seemed to be closed off by overgrown tree roots. There was a crooked sign nailed to one of the roots that said wishing well this way.

WISHING WELL THIS WAY

"I wonder where that goes," said Robecca.

Rochelle, ever the eager student, dismissed it with a shrug and quickly broke ground with her teal-colored claws. "It's not our assignment to investigate a wishing well."

"I can't believe we're getting credit to play in the dirt. It's like kindergarten all over again," Venus commented while watching Rochelle sift through a small heap of soil.

"Please don't mention kindergarten. I've always been a little jealous of ghouls who were able to actually grow up," Robecca replied quietly. "As you know, my father built me, so this is how I came into the world."

"Aha!" Rochelle squealed as she pulled an antique silver key from the ground.

"If it makes you feel any better, I think kindergarten is totally overrated," Venus consoled Robecca.

"My dad always used to say that he didn't see the point of kids going to school just to take naps and eat snacks. I really hope I get to see him again one day. . . ." Robecca trailed off.

"You will," Venus said as she wrapped her vine-covered arm around her friend.

"*Qu'est-que c'est*?" Rochelle blurted out. "I'm terribly sorry to interrupt the scarepy session, but I just found something. . . ."

"Another key?" Venus inquired.

"No, a doll," Rochelle said as she lifted a twelve-inch wooden doll from the dirt.

After delicately brushing away the soil, the three examined the coarsely carved statue that had large black eyes and a severe frown.

"I know it's been a while since I last played with dolls, but isn't this one scary-looking?" Venus muttered while inspecting the figurine carefully.

126

"Oh it's awful! It's giving me the heebie-jeebies just looking at it," Robecca muttered nervously.

"Where's Mr. Mummy? I'm most curious to hear what he'll make of it," Rochelle asked, clearly intrigued by her find.

CHAPTER nine

You are a blessed trio of ghouls to find such an artifact so early on in your archaeological careers," Mr. Mummy said with a slight hint of envy. "It took me years to find anything of such importance. Actually, if I remember correctly, my first seven months I fished out nothing but keys. . . ."

"Don't feel bad. We found a lot of those as well," Venus added reassuringly. "So, what is it?"

"A doll of doom," Mr. Mummy declared as he looked closely at the crudely carved item. "Dolls like this were historically given out by soothsayers

129

as a warning that bad luck was fast approaching."

"Great, just what we need, more signs of bad luck heading our way," Venus mumbled sarcastically.

"Mr. Mummy, my ghoulfriends are extremely superstitious, as I've come to realize most monsters are," Rochelle said, looking her teacher directly in the eye.

"You needn't worry, ghouls. White cats, white bats, dolls of doom, and even soothsayers cannot predict the future. And remember, knowledge is the cure for every curse," Mr. Mummy pontificated as though lecturing to an entire classroom of students.

"Thank you for your sage words, Mr. Mummy," Rochelle replied, pleased to have another logical mind in their midst.

"What should we do with it? Put it in the artifacts closet? Rebury it?" Robecca asked unsteadily, still frightened by the strange-looking doll.

"Mr. Mummy, I know this is a bit unorthodox, but would it be possible for me to keep it as a souvenir?" Rochelle inquired.

"I don't see why not. I already have several," Mr. Mummy replied as Venus and Robecca swallowed audibly, clearly uncomfortable with the prospect of Rochelle bringing the black-eyed figure back to their room.

Salem's Die-ner had become a popular hangout after school, almost as much as the Coffin Bean, especially for those living on campus. After all, there was only so much Creepateria food one could manage. Seated in a round booth with pink tufted cushions, Robecca, Rochelle, Venus, and Cy Clops sipped Croak-a-Cola out of black cups with bat wings for handles. Propped up conspicuously in the center of the table was the sinister-looking doll of doom.

"I realize that as a Cyclops I should be sensitive to those with ocular issues, but this doll's eyes are just plain creepy," Cy said as he pushed his half-empty plate of Crunch Cries to the side.

"I don't care what you say, Rochelle. That thing is not coming back to our room," Venus asserted firmly.

"You're acting completely ridiculous. It's just a doll, an inanimate object," Rochelle said, shaking her head incredulously at her friend.

Just then Cy reached for his Croak-a-Cola, but as he suffered from dreadful depth perception, he accidentally knocked over the doll in the process.

"Sorry, ghouls," Cy mumbled quietly.

"Don't worry," Robecca reassured him, putting her copper-colored hand on his arm, much to the boy's delight.

"*Zut!* I think it's cracked," Rochelle said as she picked up the doll. "Or is it?"

Rochelle then twisted open the figurine, exposing a small spiderweb-filled space, inside of which was a worn yellow scroll.

"What does it say?" Cy asked anxiously as Rochelle unrolled the parchment paper.

"*'You think you can trust them, but you can't,'*" Venus read over Rochelle's shoulder.

"What does that mean?" Robecca asked.

"I don't know," Venus said as she took the paper from Rochelle and lifted it to her nose. "It smells sweet, like roses and lilacs. . . ."

"May I?" Rochelle said as she pressed the parchment against her small gray nose. "It's so familiar. It must be similar to what my *grand-mère* wears."

"My bearings might be rusted, but it kind of reminds me of Miss Flapper," Robecca murmured reticently.

"Yeah, it does," Venus reluctantly agreed, her brow furrowed in concern.

"Perhaps I'm overreacting, but I think this warrants a trip to Monsieur Mummy," Rochelle pensively informed her friends.

On the way out of the Die-ner, they spotted Frankie and Draculaura at the counter, seated side by side on spiderweb-themed stools, sharing an iron shake.

"Honestly, D, I have no idea how you drink so much of this stuff," Frankie said as she dabbed the corners of her green mouth. "Hey, ghouls! Hey, Cy!"

"Frankie, Draculaura, we do not wish to interrupt your beverage intake. We just wanted to say *boojour* to our fellow Frightingales before we left to find Monsieur Mummy," Rochelle said courteously, with the doll of doom tucked beneath her arm.

"Frightingales forever!" Frankie said with a wink. "We were just talking about what we're going to do for the Hex Factor Talon Show. Can you believe it's only a couple of weeks away? Have you ghouls decided what you're doing?" Frankie asked the trio.

"Um, not yet," Robecca replied, embarrassed that they had yet to even think about the Hex Factor.

"Oh, and if you're looking for Mr. Mummy, you might want to try the Coffin Bean. I heard he's organized some kind of teachers' support group with Ms. Kindergrubber, Dr. Clamdestine, and even Mr. Hack. Apparently, they think teaching teenage monsters is super tough, but I'm like, hello, it's nowhere near as tough as *being* a teenage monster," Draculaura joked, breaking into a fang-filled smile.

Following a short walk to the Coffin Bean, Robecca, Rochelle, Venus, and Cy found that Draculaura was indeed correct: The teachers were holding a support group, or more aptly, a complaining session.

"None of them appreciates the art of cooking. That's why I want a citywide ban on all take-away food and microwavable meals. Then they'll have to learn to cook," Ms. Kindergrubber ranted, before being interrupted by Mr. Hack.

"That's nothing! I've got kids asking to borrow my mask all day long; they want to use it to scare their friends," Mr. Hack huffed.

Unsure of whether they should interrupt the meeting or wait, Rochelle ultimately made the call, remembering that the Gargoyle Code of Ethics states it's always better to voice concerns sooner rather than later.

"Gee whiz, we hate to interrupt you when you're chatting and drinking an iced blended, but could we speak to you for a quick second,

Mr. Mummy?" Robecca asked politely.

"Of course," the gauze-covered teacher stated as he rose from the table.

"We normally wouldn't bother you after school hours, but we found this note hidden inside the doll of doom. And it smells faintly of Miss Flapper's perfume," Venus explained.

Mr. Mummy took a quick glance at the parchment paper, lifted it to his nose, and then instantly shook his head.

"Ghouls, it smells like flowers. That could be anyone's perfume. Plus, it's probably been there for more than a century. Trust me, whoever it's warning us about is long gone," Mr. Mummy said, before handing back the paper and exiting the Coffin Bean with the rest of the teachers.

"For the last time, we are not having an Egyptian theme," Toralei screeched loudly, garnering the attention of everyone in the coffee shop.

"Fine, but we're not having a striped-cat theme either!" Cleo shot back furiously.

Standing a few feet away was the continuously warring duo of Toralei and Cleo, both holding iced blendeds in their hands. However, the beverages were not simply resting in their fingers but were aimed at each other like weapons.

"Babe, I want you to put down the iced blended," Deuce instructed Cleo. "You're wearing your favorite gold-gauze jumpsuit. You wouldn't want to mess that up now, would you?"

"I would rather ruin every outfit in my tomb than agree to a cat-themed Hex Factor."

"Cleo, don't talk like that. It really scares me," Deuce mumbled as he gave Clawdeen a worried look.

"Toralei? Cleo? What if you both lower your drinks at the same time?" Clawdeen suggested as she played with the tips of her finely groomed hair. "Then we'll sit down and find some kind of compromise. Maybe an Egyptian cat–themed show or perhaps nothing to do with Egypt or cats at all."

"Forget it, Clawdeen. It's never going to happen. We're only two weeks away, so we're doing it my way, which is of course the best way," Toralei stated as she raised her iced blended ever so slightly, prompting Cleo to do the same.

As the tension grew, every eye in the Coffin Bean locked on Toralei and Cleo. No one moved; no one spoke; they simply watched the school's biggest egomaniacs fight for control.

Having failed to get through to either Toralei or Cleo, Deuce and Clawdeen backed away, eager to escape the line of fire. However, as the two retreated, Jinafire approached. After hearing the commotion, the Fanghai dragon simply could not hold her tongue, or her fire, any longer.

"Excuse me, ghouls, I could not help but

overhear your dilemma. I believe an old Fanghai proverb might be of some assistance here," Jinafire interjected. "'If you fight your foes with an open heart, you might soon call them friends.'"

"Where's that from? A fortune cookie?" Toralei quipped rudely.

"More like a book on useless sayings," Cleo huffed, all the while keeping her eyes trained on Toralei.

"You are both very disrespectful and very immature," Jinafire responded, before setting Cleo and Toralei's iced blendeds ablaze, forcing the ghouls to drop them instantly.

"Ahhh! What is wrong with you?" Cleo blustered, unnerved from the sudden and entirely unexpected burst of fire.

"Seriously, are you crazy?" Toralei snapped at Jinafire. "Oh, and you can forget being asked to join the Frightingale Society, because trust me, it will never happen. And I do mean *never*."

"'Do not mess with a dragon unless you are prepared to get burned,'" Jinafire replied in an eerily calm manner.

"Talk about giving dragons a bad name," Toralei hissed.

"I do not give dragons a bad name. It is your behavior that gives monsters a bad name," Jinafire replied. "And I will have you know that only last night Miss Flapper told me what an asset I am, not only to the dragon community but to Monster High."

"Whether it's an actual spell or just some serious buttering up, Miss Flapper is definitely doing something to Skelita and Jinafire. And as usual, we haven't a clue why," Venus whispered to Robecca and Rochelle.

"*Pardonnez-moi*, Venus, just one second,"

Rochelle said, before waving Jinafire over and addressing the dragon. "While I commend your direct approach to problem solving, I must remind you that using fire indoors is very dangerous."

"I thank you for your advice, but you should know that Miss Flapper has given me the authority to use my fire as I deem necessary," Jinafire answered confidently.

The young dragon then nodded her head, smiled, and walked away.

"She's either suffering an inflated ego from all of Miss Flapper's flattery—"

"Or she's under the older dragon's control?" Rochelle interrupted Venus. "Although, if Miss Flapper is controlling the ghoul, it's not with a whisper. Jinafire isn't acting like the others did last semester."

"Well, I guess I'll just add this to the list of

things we need to figure out," Venus moaned, rife with frustration.

Meanwhile, with pools of iced blended at their feet, Cleo and Toralei continued staring venomously at each other.

"Frost my firebox, what a terrible mess! Who knew it was even possible to burn an iced blended?" Robecca blathered to Cleo and Toralei with Cy hanging right behind her. "I'd be happy to help my fellow Frightingales clean up—not that either of you have been particularly welcoming, but there's always next time."

"I can help too," Cy offered kindly, before both Cleo and Toralei turned and stalked away without so much as uttering a word.

"Or we can do it all ourselves," Robecca joked to Cy. "Not to worry, steam cleaning is my specialty."

CHAPTER
ten

later that night, while tucked comfortably in bed, Robecca, Rochelle, and Venus all found their minds wandering back to the same thing: the note inside the doll of doom. Was Mr. Mummy right? Was it merely an old relic? Or was there more to it? Was the faint scent of perfume something to be inspected?

Hours later, Rochelle's mind stirred, though the young ghoul was certain she was dreaming. There was simply no other explanation for the tightness she felt around her body; it was as though she were in a cocoon. Unable to move and surrounded by complete and utter whiteness, the gargoyle repeatedly told herself to wake up. *Wake up this instant*! But nothing happened. Irritated by her inability to stir from the dream, the grumpy gargoyle groused loudly.

"What in the name of the snail's tail has happened to our friend? She's been mummified!" Robecca squealed in her groggy morning voice.

"*Boo-la-la!* What is happening?" Rochelle called out in bewilderment.

"Hold on, Ro! I'm coming in!" Venus instructed her friend.

A sudden burst of green broke through the white wall, rescuing Rochelle from the colorless monotony. After a few seconds of pulling and pushing, Rochelle was freed from what she could now see was an elaborate spiderweb cocoon.

"I'm thinking maybe it's time to let Chewy into the hall again. Obviously, the spider population could use some controlled eatings," Venus said, before winking at her naughty, shortsighted pet plant.

"I'm surprised the bats haven't eaten the spiders," Robecca wondered aloud. "Unless, of course, they've lost the taste for them. That's what happened to me with screamed scorn. After eating it every day for a month, I suddenly stopped liking it."

"*Boo-la-la*. The stitching is simply *fangtastique*," Rochelle said, completely ignoring Robecca as she picked up a swath of the webbing and wrapped it around her neck like a scarf. "It's very chic, *n'est-ce pas*?"

So elaborate and extensive was the cocoon that hours later, while seated in Ms. Kindergrubber's Home Ick class, Rochelle was still pulling silky spider strands from her hair.

"Don't worry about the spider threads. They actually look super neat, sort of like tinsel on a normie Christmas tree. Hey, maybe that's what you should do for the Hex Factor! Dress up like a normie Christmas tree," Robecca jested while mixing together a batch of Thousand Eyelid Dressing.

"I do not find it complimentary to be compared to a normie Christmas tree," Rochelle replied as she continued to search for stray strands.

"I'm giving Howleen Wolf a Skultimate Roller Maze lesson later, if you want to tag along. After a few spirited spins around the place, every strand will have been blown off," Robecca offered with a smile.

"By the way, how are your lessons going?" Venus asked. "Draculaura mentioned that she hasn't received one complaint about you being late. I'm seriously impressed."

"Uh, um . . ." Robecca stammered.

"There is no need to stutter, Robecca. There is absolutely no shame in admitting that Cy has been escorting you to your lessons," Rochelle stated directly.

"Deary me! I didn't think you knew. I know it's silly, but I was trying to impress you ghouls, to show you that when I put my mind to it, I can arrive on time," Robecca admitted guiltily.

"You were trying to impress us? We're your ghoulfriends. Plus, there's nothing wrong with having an off internal clock," Venus explained, before raising her eyebrows. "I actually think freaky flaws kind of rule. Unless, of course, yours happens to be a desire to control the school and possibly destroy an entire crop of free-thinking young creatures."

"The desire to control or manipulate others is not a freaky flaw; it's a personality disorder," Rochelle clarified as Hoodude dashed frantically into the room, arms waving wildly in the air.

"Get back, Frankie! I'll protect you!" Hoodude shouted loudly, before throwing his body on top of the pretty green ghoul, who was seated nearby.

"Hoodude! What are you doing?" Frankie asked, stifling laughter.

However, before Hoodude could even respond, Lagoona answered Frankie's question.

"Bad luck just arrived on our doorstep. And it's looking mighty fluffy," the Mosstrailian sea creature announced while apprehensively eyeing a puffy white cat that trailed Hoodude.

"*Meow*," the furry creature with unusually large ears, supremely long whiskers, and a bubble-gum-pink nose cried.

"Is this on the record? Because I may quote you on my blog," Spectra Vondergeist, a purple-haired ghost, inquired, her chains rattling softly.

"*Meow*!" The kitten squealed again before stopping to lick its paw.

"Is that all it can say? Because *meow* isn't much of a scoop," Spectra mumbled, all the while keeping her eyes trained on the small white creature.

"Students! We must stay calm!" Ms. Kinder-grubber announced fearfully, as though she had just seen the arrival of the plague.

"Let's call in the Nami!" Hoodude hollered, still lying on top of Frankie.

"Look, I'm as superstitious as the next monster, but I'm pretty sure this is the work of Henry Hunch-back. He pulled the same thing in the Creepateria the other day," Frankie reassured the class while futilely attempting to push Hoodude off her lap.

"Good point, mate," Lagoona said, with an audible sigh of relief. "He probably dyed the critter in Mad Science just to mess with us."

As the entire room relaxed, Rochelle noticed something attached to the cat's collar and approached. It was a small piece of rolled-up parchment paper, just like the one they had found inside the doll of doom.

"*Regardez*, there's something on its collar," Rochelle whispered to Venus.

"Ms. Kindergrubber, I would like to volunteer to take this animal down to Headmistress Bloodgood's office," Venus offered politely.

"So would I!" Rochelle added.

"Me too!" Robecca chimed in.

Once the trio was safely in the hall with the kitty, Venus pulled the yellowed piece of parchment paper out from the animal's collar.

"There are spider threads on this too. Those critters certainly do get around," Venus said as she unrolled the paper.

"What does the note say?" Robecca prodded Venus impatiently.

"'*They will be our downfall.*

Just you wait,'" Venus read before lifting the paper to her nose. "Rose and lilac . . ."

"Is someone trying to warn us about Miss Flapper? And whoever she's working with?" Venus thought aloud.

"You mean the perfume is a clue to lead us to Miss Flapper?" Robecca speculated.

"Or the notes could smell of Madame Flapper because she herself is writing them?" Rochelle interjected.

"Eek! This whole thing sure does make my pistons pump!" Robecca babbled. "I know we said we weren't going to talk to Headmistress Bloodgood or Miss Sue Nami until we had concrete proof, but I think we need to rethink that."

"I agree. I vote for Miss Sue Nami. She's always been more suspicious of Miss Flapper," Venus responded.

A light sprinkling of rain blanketed the luscious lawns of Monster High, making the green stalks of grass shimmer in the faint afternoon light.

"Where is Miss Sue Nami? I'll start rusting if I stay out here any longer," Robecca whined from beneath her umbrella.

"There she is," Venus called out, spotting Miss Nami, along with three trolls, working diligently to remove a large banner from the wrought-iron fence that surrounded the school.

"Miss Sue Nami, we really need to speak with you—" Venus started, before being unceremoniously cut off by the brash woman.

"If you see Hoodude, tell him he has detention in the no-fungeon *forever*," Miss Sue Nami barked as the trolls pulled down the I ❤ FRANKIE STEIN poster.

"No heart anymore," one of the trolls grunted before ripping the banner in half.

"Non-adult entities, it's against school policy to skip class, so I'm going to have to ask you all to accompany me to the no-fungeon for mandatory detention."

"That's absolutely fine with me. Anything to get out of the rain," Robecca whimpered.

Once safely back in the main corridor, Venus explained that they had Ms. Kindergrubber's permission to leave class and transport the white cat to her.

"If that's true, non-adult entity, then where is the cat?" Miss Sue Nami inquired aggressively.

"As my ghoulfriends are a bit superstitious, I placed the cat in my satchel," Rochelle explained and then pulled out the small, puffy ball of fur.

"Normally the sight of a white cat causes my skin to crawl and my legs to shake, but seeing as this is nothing more than a prank courtesy of Henry Hunchback, I couldn't care less," Miss Sue Nami declared, before turning to a troll. "But nevertheless, get that feline off campus."

"Miss Sue Nami, we think there's more to the cat. We recently came across a couple of ominous notes, both of which smelled faintly of Miss Flapper's perfume," Robecca explained.

"Stop right there. This is the work of a prankster, nothing more. So quit imagining trouble where there isn't any and get back to class," Miss Sue Nami instructed firmly and then stormed off down the hall.

Still damp from their trek outside, Robecca, Rochelle, and Venus decided it was wise to quickly change clothes before returning to class. However, just as they turned down the dormitory corridor, they noted the unmistakable silhouette of Miss Flapper outside their door.

"Madame Flapper," Rochelle said, startling the dragon, "is there something we can help you with?"

"Oh no, I was simply coming by to see if you might join me for tea after school," Miss Flapper explained. "I just picked up some delicious blueberry crones."

"Thanks, but we have a lot of homework to do," Venus responded in a less-than-friendly tone.

"I must say, Madame Flapper, I am most surprised you would come by at this hour to ask us for tea. After all, it's the middle of the school day," Rochelle pointed out, her suspicion clearly piqued.

"Normally I wouldn't, but I just received an e-mail from Jinafire saying that the three of you had left Home Ick early. So I thought now might be a good time to ask you," Miss Flapper said softly, before floating gracefully into her room.

"Jinafire is spying on us, keeping Miss Flapper

abreast of our comings and goings," Venus whispered upon entering the Chamber of Gore and Lore.

"*Boo-la-la*, this is most disconcerting," Rochelle mumbled dejectedly. "It appears Jinafire and Skelita are most definitely under her control."

After changing into dry clothes, the trio made its way down the creaky pink staircase en route back to Ms. Kindergrubber's class. However, they were quickly distracted by a sudden jolt permeating the walls.

"What was that?" Venus asked Robecca and Rochelle while motioning for them to follow her into the hall.

Standing in the middle of the main corridor, surrounded by a plethora of trolls, was Miss

Sue Nami, looking absolutely irate. So livid was the waterlogged woman that she was actually foaming at the mouth. And upon inching closer, the trio noticed that the trolls were not simply surrounding Miss Sue Nami but holding her back, stopping her from throwing her "wave" against the wall again.

Just as Robecca opened her copper-plated lips to inquire about what was happening, she spotted the large black letters scrawled across the lockers. The message, like the others she had seen, was short and to the point: THEY ARE WATCHING YOU.

"Vandalism is against school policy!" Miss Sue Nami shrieked angrily.

"Miss Sue Nami, you must calm down! I fear your head might fly off your body, and while that is a common occurrence for me, the same cannot be said for you," Headmistress Bloodgood cautioned as she looked at the graffiti. "Although I certainly

159

understand your fury toward this prankster."

"Someone get me Henry Hunchback!" Miss Sue Nami hollered.

"He home sick today, no him," one of the trolls grunted in response.

"I always thought pranks were contagious, and now I have proof!" Miss Sue Nami shouted. "And when I find out who did this, I am going to suspend them, ban them from taking part in next week's Hex Factor Talon Show, and sentence them to cleaning the trolls' quarters!"

It wasn't long before the school's biggest blogger, Spectra Vondergeist, had picked up the story, going so far as to name the anonymous culprit Pranksy. Within days, a new phenomenon known as Pranksy Guessing was sweeping the school.

Students spent every free moment trying to guess the identity of the mythical scribbler. And as the number of messages increased so did the curiosity surrounding Pranksy.

"What is wrong with our classmates and teachers?" Venus asked her roommates with understandable frustration while listening to a bunch of nearby creatures babble about Pranksy. "How can they possibly believe this Pranksy nonsense? Do they really think this is all the work of some secret artist?"

"I heard that some of the pumpkin heads are even planning on singing a song about Pranksy at the Hex Factor Talon Show," Robecca said, shaking her head incredulously.

"Sadly, the Pranksy situation can be summed up quite simply," Rochelle stated somberly. "Those who don't remember the past are doomed to repeat it."

CHAPTER
eleven

"no more meow! No meow!"

"Bad kitty! Bad kitty!"

"This way! No, this way!"

"Cat deaf? Why no listen?"

It was a terribly amusing thing to see: trolls herding cats in the halls. Cats, much like trolls themselves, do not listen to anyone; they change their minds at the slightest whim, and they generally look to please themselves before anyone else. So it was hardly a surprise that cat herding had become a most irksome addition to the trolls' workload. But in light of the sheer number of white felines appearing on campus each day, cat herding was an undeniably necessary part of patrolling the halls.

After removing the small parchment notes from the cats' collars, the trolls then released them at the edge of town. Unsure how to handle the feline epidemic, Headmistress Bloodgood had created a plan, dubbed Normie Loves Fluffy, whereby the animals were taken to shelters in neighboring normie towns. As normies were very fond of fluffy cats, especially white ones they could name Snowball, Headmistress Bloodgood considered this to be a very sound solution.

"Trick! Treat!" Rochelle hollered. "There you are! Deuce and I waited almost twenty-five minutes for you two. Did you forget you had a tutoring session?"

"The cats! The cats!" Trick cried.

"Cats everywhere!" Treat hollered, before the

two took off after a rogue kitten.

"Not a pretty sight, is it?" Deuce joked as they watched Trick and Treat waddle away.

"At least they're getting some exercise. Now if the cats could only teach them to clean themselves," Rochelle teased.

"I wouldn't hold your breath," Deuce said warmly, patting Rochelle on the arm before greeting a fast-approaching Cleo.

While the sheer touch of his hand still gave Rochelle's cold granite skin goose bumps, she wasn't quite as madly infatuated with Deuce as she had been previously. In part because she had come to see that just as Mr. D'eath liked to be down, Deuce liked to be bossed around by Cleo.

"Bye, Deuce. Bye, Cleo," Rochelle called out as she heard the soft *ping* of her iCoffin in her pocket. After pulling out the device, she paused, then wrinkled her brow and darted off down the hall.

Upon returning to the Chamber of Gore and Lore, Rochelle found Robecca and Venus lounging on their beds, reading the latest gossip about Pranksy on Spectra's blog. As the messages and cats had continued popping up around campus, the enthusiasm for Pranksy had multiplied. So intrigued was the student body by the mythical monster, they had all but forgotten that the Hex Factor Talon Show was now only days away.

"Ghouls, today is Day of the Dad! I might have completely forgotten if not for the help of my trusty iCoffin. It really does keep me organized," Rochelle proclaimed happily.

"That's funny. My iCoffin doesn't keep me organized.

Maybe I need a new one?" Robecca pondered.

"I can't believe it's Day of the Dad already. I bet Pops is sitting by the pond, knee-deep in soil and enjoying the sun," Venus imagined with a smile. "Nothing like a little photosynthesis," she continued, before picking up her iCoffin to call home.

As Venus cheerfully spoke to her father, Rochelle cautiously dialed her parents' number, taking special care not to let her claws crack the screen of her iCoffin.

With both her roommates chatting away happily, Robecca experienced something she hadn't felt in a long time—homesickness. She missed her father. Just imagining his kind face made her eyes prick with tears, which promptly turned to steam. Not wanting to rain, or more aptly steam, on the others' parades, Robecca quietly crept out of the room.

Longing to see her father, or even just feel connected to him, Robecca went to the only place she could think of that reminded her of him—the catacombs. Alone in the elevator, Robecca's eyes steamed uncontrollably as she wondered if her father had become mechanical, allowing him to live on, albeit differently.

Stepping off the elevator, Rochelle wiped away pools of condensation on her cheeks before noting that half the letters on the welcome sign were now obscured by lacy spiderwebs. *Miss Sue Nami really needs to get on top of the arachnid situation*, Robecca thought, before wondering why she hadn't actually seen any spiders, just their webs. How was that possible? Perhaps the spiders had found a means to traverse campus without being seen, she speculated.

Wandering the many dimly lit tunnels of the catacombs, Robecca thought of all the things she longed to speak with her father about: joining the Frightingale Society, her ghoulfriends, Skultimate Roller Maze, and most obviously about what was happening at Monster High.

A sudden burst of perfume walloped Robecca's olfactory drive, instantly causing her breath to shorten and her ears to steam. And it was not because the scent was unpleasant or laced with some sort of dangerous chemical. It was simply the familiar aroma of Miss Flapper's perfume, a delightful mix of lilac and rose. But as this was an odor Robecca associated with duplicity and even, to some degree, danger, experiencing it so intensely had quite a negative effect on the young ghoul. Leaning against the wall, next to Scarisian politician Charles de Ghoul's fluorescent purple portrait, Robecca cringed painfully. The scent appeared to be physically ailing the ghoul, almost as if sand were being poured into her gears.

"I can't believe how insensitive we were. Seriously, what is wrong with us?" Venus moaned to Rochelle, before throwing her head into her soft green hands.

"I must agree, even by blunt gargoyle standards, that was very dense of me to simply announce that it was Day of the Dad without even considering her situation," Rochelle lamented as Penny glared menacingly at her, prompting the guilty gargoyle to quickly look away.

"We need to find Robecca. Can you imagine how sad she must feel right now? Ugh! I am so mad at myself. I deserve to be sneezed on a thousand times over. Absolutely nothing makes me gloomier than a friend being down except, of course, the environment being weighed down with chemical pollutants."

"Venus, *s'il ghoul plaît*, let's try to stay on track here. We haven't time to discuss environmental concerns. Now let's think, where could she be? She's not allowed in Cy's room. Do you think she might have gone to see Skelita and Jinafire?"

"No way. She knows that they might have fallen under Miss Flapper's control," Venus replied before pausing. "Unless, of course, that's *why* she went to see them, to try to get more information about their relationship with Miss Flapper."

"*Boo-la-la*, solo investigations are never a good idea. We'd better go!"

CHAPTER

twelve

rochelle tapped her freshly polished pink claws against the door to the Chamber of Hairy and Scary, leaving small, almost imperceptible dents in their wake. The muffled sound of ghouls laughing traveled through the thick door, offering both Rochelle and Venus much-needed encouragement on their quest to find Robecca.

"Come in," Jinafire called out loudly.

Venus flung open the door to the Chamber of Hairy and Scary with such gusto that she almost lost a vine in the process.

173

"Hello, ghouls," a soft and rapturous voice beckoned from the corner of the tidy dorm room. "I just arrived with tea and crones. Would you care to join us?"

Lounging stylishly in a long silk kimono was none other than Miss Flapper—only she wasn't alone; she had two trolls sitting at her feet like guard dogs.

"*Sí, sí*, please join us. We're having a tea party," Skelita said warmly. "And later I'm going to show Miss Flapper how to do her makeup à la Day of the Dead. I can do yours too if you'd like."

"Actually, we're looking for Robecca. Have you ghouls seen her?"

"Venus, you look a bit worried. Has something happened?" Miss Flapper asked tenderly, absolutely brimming with concern.

"No, she's fine. We're just looking for her," Venus replied stiffly.

"I am very sorry to tell you, but I have not seen Robecca all day," Jinafire said while fiddling with the green wisps at the end of her golden tail.

"Are you sure you ghouls can't stay?" Miss Flapper inquired. "The trolls give excellent foot rubs."

"*Boo-la-la*! I do not find that very enticing," Rochelle replied candidly, imagining the trolls' filth-laden hands touching her well-polished feet.

"Well then, perhaps another time. Don't forget, I'm just next door."

"Trust me, Miss Flapper, we won't," Venus said honestly—perhaps too honestly, judging by the look on the teacher's face.

After finally escaping the anxiety-inducing fog of perfume, Robecca veered into Mr. Mummy's classroom, a shortcut to the catacombs' elevator.

While walking between the brightly colored desks, she suddenly paused, paralyzed by what she saw. Scrawled across the wall in fluorescent pink paint was yet another message:

YOU DIDN'T LISTEN. NOW IT'S TOO LATE. WE'RE ALL DOOMED!

"Deary me! Deary me!" Robecca mumbled to herself as she ran toward the elevator, desperate to tell someone about what she'd found.

As the elevator doors opened into the main corridor, a flummoxed Robecca ran straight into Spectra Vondergeist. Ever the diligent reporter, the purple-haired ghost was once again in the process of uploading a blog post from her iCoffin.

"What's the rush, ghoulfriend? Got a story? Want to share?" Spectra asked Robecca with a raised eyebrow and a curious smile.

"In the name of the bird's beak! There's another message!"

"Outside the Mad and Deranged Scientist Laboratory? I know. I'm just finishing up my blog post on it. I must say, Pranksy really keeps himself busy."

"The Mad and Deranged Scientist Laboratory? I was talking about the catacombs!" Robecca explained before pausing. "Wait, what does the message by the Mad and Deranged Scientist Laboratory say?"

"Sorry, ghoul. You're going to have to read my blog to find out," Spectra said with a smile before floating away.

Without waiting a beat, Robecca pulled out her iCoffin, desperate to read Spectra's blog.

"'*Pranksy, Monster High's most notorious graffitist, has struck again, and this time he's made a very powerful enemy—Mr. Hack,*'" Robecca read out loud. "'*Pranksy scrawled* they will be our demise *and* they will be the end of us *on the floor in front of the Mad and Deranged Scientist Laboratory. And Mr. Hack has promised to fail Pranksy once his or her identity has been revealed. Stay tuned. . . . Oh, and don't forget your umbrella. It looks like it's going to rain again this afternoon.'*"

Robecca stuffed her iCoffin in her pocket and then darted down the hall toward the dormitory.

The black-and-blue-haired ghoul was just about halfway up the rose-colored staircase when she found herself face-to-face with the always well-groomed Miss Flapper. With the long silk kimono clinging perfectly to her frame, the European dragon was rather breathtaking.

"Just the ghoul I was looking for," Miss Flapper hissed slowly.

"You're looking for me? Do you need something steamed? While I am of course happy to do it,

I'm nowhere near as good as a real dry cleaner, especially right now, since my pressure gauge is acting up," Robecca babbled while fiddling clumsily with one of her rivets.

"Steam something? I would never ask you such a thing. Actually, I was looking for you because I heard from Abbey Bominable that you're an excellent Skultimate Roller Maze teacher. So I thought I might take you up on your offer for free lessons. Maybe afterward we could even grab a Croak-a-Cola at the Die-ner."

Robecca smiled and racked her brain for an acceptable excuse, but she simply could not think of one.

"Gee whiz, that sounds swell. Really truly swell, but . . ." Robecca trailed off. "Unfortunately I am so bogged down with homework, I've had to suspend my Skultimate Roller Maze tutorials," she continued as she inelegantly tried to pass the dragon on the stairs.

Now only a few inches from the delicate creature, Robecca once again smelled the familiar mixture of lilac and rose, prompting her pistons to stall. Uncomfortable and anxious, Robecca summoned all the water she had left in her boiler to push past the dainty dragon.

"Well, maybe next time," Miss Flapper said with palpable disappointment.

"Toodles!" Robecca blurted out as she pushed aside the webbed curtain and zoomed down the dormitory hall before coming to a screeching halt. There, positioned just before her door, was Penny with a note tied tightly around her neck.

Oh dear, oh dear, Robecca thought. *They've gotten to Penny!*

Unable to face reading the note alone, Robecca immediately turned to go in search of Rochelle and Venus, whom she promptly found right behind her. As Robecca tried to explain what she had discovered, Rochelle and Venus interrupted her repeatedly to say they'd been looking for her everywhere so they could apologize for their Day of the Dad insensitivity.

"Oh, enough about Day of the Dad! Can we please stay focused on Penny?" Robecca hollered, pointing at the floor.

"Let's get her inside," Venus said as she picked up the sour-faced penguin and opened the door to the Chamber of Gore and Lore.

After removing the note and silently reading it to herself, Venus paused, prompting Rochelle to clear her throat theatrically. "Venus, you must read the note *aloud*.

Honestly, look at poor Robecca. She's on the verge of blowing a gasket!"

Venus nodded and then pursed her lips before finally reading the note. "'*Dear Robecca, I just wanted to see how you were doing. I'm leaving this note with Penny, but as she looks deeply annoyed by both Roux and Chewy, I'm going to put her in the hall for a little peace and quiet. Your friend, Cy.*'"

"Oh, I've never been happier to hear from that one-eyed wonder in my life!" Robecca squealed as she engulfed Penny in a massive hug.

"Ve vould have taken his message, but ve vere just too tired," a voice came from beneath Rochelle's bed.

"Oh, come on! Not again," Venus groaned as Rose and Blanche Van Sangre crept out from under Rochelle's and Robecca's beds.

"*Boo-la-la*! Why are you so obsessed with our room?" Rochelle inquired as she shook her head and tapped her fingers in frustration atop a nearby table.

"Ve vere asleep in the Libury, but Cleo and Toralei vere screaming so loudly, ve couldn't get a moment's rest," Blanche said as she wiped sleep from her eyes.

"Those two have gone completely batty over the Hex Factor. It's only a few days away, and they still can't agree on a theme. Honestly, if I were Frankie or Draculaura, I would have tossed them out of the Frightingale Society after the way they have behaved," Robecca commented with a judgmental air.

"No, this time zey veren't fighting about the Hex Factor, zey vere hollering about how much zey hated ze rain, that it's ruining zeir hair," Rose explained as she grabbed hold of her sister's arm.

After exchanging seemingly blank expressions with each other, Rose and Blanche exited the room without offering so much as a "sorry" or "thank you."

"Well, I finally have something in common with Cleo and Toralei. I also hate the rain," Venus confided to the others.

"What? How can an environmentalist hate the rain?" Robecca asked with a perplexed expression.

"It's kind of hard to maintain a neat and tidy compost pile when the rain keeps washing everything away. I hate to admit it, but the back field is starting to look like a trash dump." Venus sighed dejectedly.

"In that case, I think it might be wise for you and Lagoona to put the pile on hold until after the storm passes," Rochelle suggested.

"Ugh, failure. It's more exhausting than I thought it would be. I'm going to bed," Venus complained as she crawled beneath her sheets.

Early the next morning Robecca popped out of bed screaming, "What time is it? What time is it?"

"Go back to bed," Venus groaned from under her mummy-gauze and werewolf-fur sheets. "The sun isn't even out yet."

"Actually, Venus, the sun is out; it's just hidden behind all these terrible black rain clouds. For once Robecca is actually on time," Rochelle explained as their morning alarm clock started to beep.

"Did you hear that, Penny? I'm on time! Deary me! I'm so happy, I could do three laps around the school!"

"Cool your jets, Robecca," Venus grumbled. "If you do three laps around the school, then you'll miss breakfast and most likely be seriously late for Catacombing class."

The three sleepy-eyed ghouls had only just sat down in the Creepateria when Lagoona came rushing up to their table with a muddy piece of paper in hand.

"Venus, I've been looking all over for you!" Lagoona said excitedly. "I went out to the compost pile this morning to spread some dirt over it, ya know, to contain things until after the storm passes. Only I didn't even have a chance to do that because look what I found pinned to an old apple core," she finished, handing Venus the filth-laden note.

"'*Ticktock, ticktock. Your freedom is about to disappear. They're almost here,*'" Venus said, reading the letter aloud.

"And Gil and Ghoulia just found notes in their lockers. I've got to say, this whole Pranksy thing is getting kind of creepy," Lagoona confessed. "And not in a good way."

"You can say that again," Venus said as she discreetly sniffed the letter and then nodded to Robecca and Rochelle to convey the presence of perfume. "Come on, ghouls, Pranksy or no Pranksy, we're going to be late for Catacombing if we don't get a move on it."

"We need to figure out whether the notes are about Miss Flapper or written by her," Venus explained seriously to Rochelle and Robecca as they sifted carefully through soil at their digging station in Catacombing class.

"The fact that the notes, cats, and messages are increasing in number tells us that something is coming. That trouble is fast approaching,"

Rochelle hypothesized as she pulled another antique key from the ground.

"Jeez Louise, how many keys did our forefathers need? They must have locked up everything," Robecca said as she played with the old rusted key.

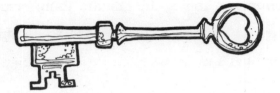

"Maybe we should make jewelry out of them. They're kind of ghoul," Venus suggested, holding up a couple of keys to see how they would look.

"Wear something rusty? That's less appealing than listening to Toralei and Cleo fight about the Hex Factor," Robecca replied candidly.

"Speaking of which, the Hex Factor's almost here, so I'm guessing we're not participating," Venus surmised.

"As far as I am concerned, clapping at the

end of each act is a valid form of participation," Rochelle stated sincerely.

"Ahhhhh! Help me! Help me!" Frankie Stein's voice echoed through the tunnels, prompting all who heard it to run back to the classroom.

Standing in the middle of the room was Mr. Mummy, inspecting a letter covered in spider threads that had been found inside another doll of doom.

"What does it say?" Venus asked Draculaura.

"*How can you sit here and dig through the past while they destroy the future?*" Draculaura responded. "But that's not all. Just as she opened it, a stone came crashing down from the ceiling. It only missed her by an inch. I don't care what anyone says. These dolls bring bad luck. I mean, look what just happened to Frankie."

"Boys and ghouls, I have some business to

attend to with the headmistress. Therefore, I have no choice but to dismiss class early. Please pack up your tools and head for the elevator," Mr. Mummy said, directing his students.

"Dolls cannot bring bad luck," Rochelle whispered intently to her ghoulfriends. "The stone falling was nothing more than an unfortunate coincidence."

"Whether they bring bad luck or not, at least someone's starting to realize this isn't a prank," Venus muttered with relief.

Using what Robecca, Rochelle, and Venus could only imagine was her ghostly nature, Spectra managed to "overhear" Mr. Mummy's conversation with the headmistress and Miss Sue Nami. After weeks of dismissing the notes and cats as nothing more than pranks, they had come to realize that Monster High was in actual danger. But since they didn't know who the notes were warning them about or who had written them, they hadn't a clue as to the proper course of action.

Within minutes of hearing this, Spectra updated her blog, declaring that there was in fact no Pranksy and that the school was currently facing great peril. The blog post dramatically altered the mood in the halls, filling students and staff members alike with all-consuming anxiety about the future.

The stressful atmosphere only intensified when monster after monster discovered dolls of doom in their lockers, each containing an ominous note warning of the mysterious *they*. But worst of all, the dolls were now universally accepted to be messengers of bad luck. And whether real or imagined, those who received the dolls felt terrible things were occurring to them immediately after coming into contact with the coarsely carved figurines.

"*Ahhh!*" Cleo screeched as she threw a doll of doom at Deuce. "Get rid of it!"

"What? No! I don't want to touch it! Don't you remember what happened last time? No more than two hours after holding a doll of doom, I accidentally turned that bird to stone," Deuce responded, ducking as the doll flew past him.

"You're complaining about turning a bird into stone? One day after I found that doll in the Creepateria, I ripped my favorite gauze leggings! Do you even understand how important gauze is to a mummy? It's like fur to a werewolf or fangs to a vampire!"

"Ouch!" Draculaura whimpered as she tried to remove a large splinter she received while handling the rough wooden doll of doom. "Two seconds after touching it, and I'm already in pain."

"*Boo-la-la*, everyone is becoming hysterical. They've lost the ability to rationally see what's happening," Rochelle said as she shook her head.

"I'm more worried about the steady increase of dolls. It feels like they're building up to something," Venus whispered to Rochelle and Robecca as they made their way down the corridor to G-ogre-phy.

"Yes, and I only wish we knew what. Then we might have a chance to stop it," Rochelle said somberly.

"Deary me! Deary me!" Robecca blathered

193

nervously as small bursts of steam escaped her ears.

"Non-adult entities, I would like to have a minute of your time in private." Miss Sue Nami splashed into view and motioned for the trio to follow her.

"While we would be more than happy to speak with you, we do not wish to be late for G-ogre-phy. Tardiness is against the rules and, as you know, I take rules very seriously, Miss Sue Nami," Rochelle proclaimed earnestly, much to the Deputy of Disaster's delight.

"I respect your rule-abiding nature and will personally explain your tardiness to your teacher. Now follow me," Miss Sue Nami grunted, heading toward the Study Howl.

Miss Sue Nami looked nervously around the room, scanning every nook and cranny for possible eavesdroppers.

"I need some information," Miss Sue Nami said in an abnormally quiet voice.

"Unfortunately, Miss Sue Nami, we do not have solid evidence as to who is behind the notes, cats, and dolls, but to be frank, we do have our suspicions about a certain someone," Rochelle interjected, before giving the soggy woman a chance to even ask her question.

"As you are aware, I no longer believe this to be the work of a prankster. And therefore I have started investigating," Miss Sue Nami leaned in and whispered conspiratorially. "Headmistress Bloodgood might have wholeheartedly believed Miss Flapper when she claimed to be under a spell last semester, but I didn't. You have to get up pretty early in the morning to fool the Deputy of Disaster."

"Actually, getting up early in the morning has nothing to do with fooling people," Rochelle corrected the waterlogged woman.

"Rochelle, it's a figure of speech," Venus explained, and then motioned for Miss Sue Nami to continue.

"Well, seeing as you non-adult entities are currently living next door to that crafty-eyed clotheshorse, I thought you might have seen something."

"*Seen* something? No. Heard something? Yes," Venus replied.

"What do you mean?" Miss Sue Nami asked impatiently.

"Shortly into the semester we heard someone crawl across our ceiling and jump down into Miss Flapper's room. And then we heard her angrily tell off the visitor for coming to see her and putting her plan in jeopardy," Venus explained.

"What did she say the plan was?"

"She didn't," Rochelle responded, "which is

why I think it's wise we follow her movements a bit more closely," Rochelle added while Miss Sue Nami jumped up from the table, nodded her head, and stormed out of the room, leaving many a puddle in her wake.

CHAPTER
thirteen

tucked snugly behind a large wooden planter's box at Ms. Kindergrubber's Garden for Grub, Robecca ran her smooth copper fingers through the grass. The soft strands tickled her hand, instantly distracting the young ghoul. No longer focused on watching Miss Flapper through the weathered wooden slats, Robecca daydreamed of curling up on the lush lawn for a quiet nap. It was an odd thought, seeing as how Robecca, unlike the Van Sangre sisters, did not much care for sleeping in public places, or anywhere other than her bed, for that matter.

199

 But so inviting were the silky stalks, she completely forgot about Miss Flapper, who was currently gathering small white daisies in a wicker basket.

It was a rather idyllic scene: A beautiful young dragon picking flowers in a wonderfully lush garden. Except for the part about the three young ghouls carefully monitoring her every move for any sign of impropriety.

"I can't believe she's picking flowers. Who actually does that?" Venus whispered seconds after scurrying over to Rochelle.

"*Évidemment*, Madame Flapper does, but I suspect many other monsters do as well, especially those with gardens," Rochelle replied while Venus simultaneously rolled her eyes and shook her head at the preternaturally literal gargoyle.

"Rusty gears!" Robecca hissed, having only just

looked up from the grass. "The Winged Wonder is on the move," she continued, pointing to Miss Flapper sashaying gracefully toward the garden's main gate.

"Winged Wonder? I thought we decided her code name was Red Robin?" Venus questioned Robecca.

"Why are you two so insistent on having a code name for her? She has a perfectly good real name, which everyone remembers," Rochelle pointed out logically.

"Rochelle, why don't we just cut off the snail's tail while we're at it?" Robecca snapped.

"And before you say it, yes, we know snails don't actually have tails! Robecca's just trying to say that having a code name makes the mission a little more fun, and it helps us forget that we are once again chasing Miss Flapper as our school faces some kind of . . . something!" Venus huffed.

"Very well then. I vote for Curiously Couture," Rochelle remarked with an approving nod, clearly pleased with her choice.

"Jeepers, the name debate is going to have to wait. We need to move," Robecca whispered as Miss Flapper exited the indoor garden seconds before the trio discreetly scampered after her into the school's main building.

As the academic day had only just ended an hour before, the corridors were still lively with monsters making their way to after-school clubs. Most surprisingly, even with the rampant anxiety coursing through the halls, students dutifully tended to their activities: everything from Skultimate Roller Maze practice to preparing for the Hex Factor Talon Show, which was now just about here.

After kicking a couple of crumpled notes out of the way, Robecca, Rochelle, and Venus continued trailing Miss Flapper, using a group of trolls as cover.

In the days since the white cats, ominous notes, and dolls of doom had started appearing all over campus, the trolls' workload had increased exponentially. The bulky beasts had always looked less than spooktacular with their greasy locks and dirty smudges, yet now they appeared ragged and worn down in a way they never had before. As a matter of fact, so tremendous was their labor that there had even been rumors of a troll strike. Fortunately, Miss Sue Nami had suppressed their growing desire to unionize by promising to throw an epic two-day Troll Appreciation Feast filled with everything from ghoulash to pus pastries.

"*Zut!* These trolls are too slow," Rochelle complained as they ducked behind Jackson Jekyll and Three-Headed Freddie.

"Good golly, Three-Headed Freddie's never been quite so helpful," Robecca said with a giggle.

After carefully hopping from one cluster of students to another, Robecca, Rochelle, and Venus managed to successfully follow Miss Flapper all the way to the Libury unseen.

The dark and dusty space was absolutely brimming with studious young monsters desperately trying to finish their work while threats of unknown entities loomed on the horizon.

In an effort to fit in and deflect any attention, Robecca, Rochelle, and Venus each picked up a book.

"Don't get too close," Robecca instructed as Venus stayed on Miss Flapper's tail, weaving in and out of the book-filled stacks.

"I want to see what book she took," Venus replied. "It could be important."

"*Regardez!* She's talking to Jinafire and Skelita," Rochelle whispered.

"Talking? Or meeting up?" Venus asked pointedly.

"I must say, they seem closer than a bee to its honey, and that is not a good thing," Robecca added.

"Robecca? Robecca? Hey, Robecca?" a voice cut through the quiet room.

"And our cover is blown," Venus droned with frustration as everyone in earshot—including Miss Flapper, Jinafire, and Skelita—turned to see who was calling Robecca's name.

"Oh hello, Cy," Robecca quietly greeted the boy, realizing that their covert mission had just failed most unceremoniously.

"What are you doing with a book called *Trollogy: Astrology for Trolls*?" he asked, looking down at the tome in Robecca's hands.

"She picked it up in an attempt to blend in while

following Miss Flapper through the Libury, which was working quite successfully until you called her name so loudly," Venus explained, all the while following Miss Flapper with her eyes.

"I'm really sorry, ghouls. I had no idea. I just wanted to say hi to Robecca," Cy said sheepishly. "So, um, hi."

"Hi," Robecca replied with a rueful smile.

"I can't take it! Dis is third one dis week!" Abbey Bominable groaned as she pulled a doll of doom from her backpack while seated at a nearby table. "And now I'm already starting to feel hot. Fevers are very dangerous for yetis! When is dis all going to stop?"

"Probably when 'they' arrive," Draculaura replied nervously to Abbey. "This whole thing has left me so jittery, I can't even drink my shakes. Instead, I actually *have* the shakes!"

"Everyone's pretty stressed out, huh?" Cy commented to Robecca.

"Understandably. All this anticipation is making me want to squeak louder than a rusted joint," Robecca replied as steam slowly exited her ears.

"Robecca, you must calm down or your hair's going to be absolutely bananas, and like you always say . . ." Rochelle warned her friend in a maternal tone.

"Bananas might be good for cereal, but they're not good for a monster's hair," Robecca finished.

"Actually," Rochelle started, "you can mash them up and—"

"Red Robin or the Winged Wonder or Curiously Couture . . . Oh forget it! Miss Flapper is on the move," Venus interrupted, watching the graceful dragon make her way to the Libury door.

"Leave the books. We don't have time to

properly check them out," Rochelle instructed the others seriously. "On second thought, Cy, might I ask you to reshelve them? It feels like a violation of Libury policy to simply leave them here."

"Of course," Cy replied quietly while nodding his head.

"That's so nice of you, Cy," Robecca gushed, before looking over at the checkout counter. "Especially since the liburian seems absolutely *buried* in work," she remarked while being pulled away by Rochelle and Venus.

Once back in the hall, the trio continued moving between clusters of students, doing their absolute best to stay off Miss Flapper's radar. However, upon turning the corner and coming face-to-face with the school's two fiercest ghouls, they paused.

"Ugh, the smell of your gauze makes me want to gag," Toralei said, making a most unflattering sound, like that of dislodging a hair ball.

"Oh really? Well, I've been waiting all day to tell you that your outfit is a serious *cata*strophe," Cleo shot back ferociously as Miss Flapper sauntered by the warring monsters without so much as a word.

"What kind of teacher ignores ghouls fighting?" Venus asked the others.

"Considering who's fighting, I would say a smart one," Robecca replied as Miss Flapper opened the door to the east wing.

"So much for following her; she's headed back to the dorms," Venus moaned disappointedly.

"Speaking of which, we ought to get back there as well. Homework must still be done, even in the face of great uncertainty," Rochelle stated stoically.

"Jeepers, Rochelle, you make it sound like we're going to war," Robecca babbled as they made their way toward the dormitory.

"I still can't believe that woman was picking flowers," Venus said, with a notable air of judgment.

"Venus, it seems like flower picking is a pretty sensitive subject for you. Is there something you'd like to share?" Robecca asked sincerely.

"Since you asked, I think the senseless murder of flowers for decoration is plain wrong! Why kill them when they can live in a nice potted plant like Chewy?" Venus proclaimed passionately as she stomped up the rickety pink staircase, now a mere ten feet behind Miss Flapper.

"I see your point about flowers. It does seem rather senseless and illogical, especially since potted flowers would last a great deal longer," Rochelle acquiesced.

"Oh!" Miss Flapper cried out in shock before turning toward Robecca, Rochelle, and Venus. "Oh, ghouls, it's terrible! You've been hit!"

"By an asteroid?" Robecca blurted out nonsensically.

"Rochelle, have you gone mad? *Complètement folle*? Why are you talking about asteroids?"

"Gee whiz, I don't know. Sometimes when I'm on edge, I just blurt out the first thing that comes to my mind," the copper-plated girl blathered as small wisps of steam escaped her ears.

"I'm terribly sorry to have confused you. I simply meant they left a message on your door," Miss Flapper explained softly.

Venus read the writing on the door to the Chamber of Gore and Lore aloud. "'*It's time for you to know who they are.*'"

CHAPTER
fourteen

good morning, ghouls and boys! It's going to be another wet and stormy day here at Monster High. And I'm not just talking about the weather. Last night the dormitory chamber of Robecca Steam, Venus McFlytrap, and Rochelle Goyle was vandalized with the following message: IT'S TIME FOR YOU TO KNOW WHO THEY ARE. Could it be that the trio involved in ending last semester's monster whisper knows "who they are"? Do they know more than they are letting on? Inquiring monsters want to know. Oh, and don't forget your galoshes—the rain continues!

213

"Spectra's a nice ghoul. Why doesn't she realize that she's planting seeds of doubt about us in our classmates' minds?" Venus huffed, before tossing the iCoffin onto her unmade bed.

"Spectra sees herself as a journalist whose job it is to report what she finds," Rochelle explained. "It's not personal."

"Well, it sure feels personal," Venus blustered.

"In the name of the bird's beak! I do believe your nose is twitching and your eyes are watering," Robecca noted as she stepped back. "Are you going to sneeze? Because orange really doesn't suit me; copper is a very difficult color to coordinate with."

"Venus, *s'il ghoul plaît*, you must calm down. It's a couple silly lines. And it's not such a big deal to imply that we might know more than we are letting on. It's not as if she accused us of being *them*," Rochelle remarked in her usual logical way.

"Ah, I guess that's true," Venus acquiesced as an earsplitting thunderclap ripped through the sky. "I feel like it's been raining forever. It's starting to make me crazy."

"Excessive periods of rain have been known to cause hatred for weather reporters, slipping, and mold due to dampness—so crazy is not totally out of the realm of possibility," Rochelle pronounced as though she were a medical professional. "Now then, I think it's time we get to the Creepateria for breakfast."

As Robecca, Rochelle, and Venus walked down the main corridor, they sensed that something was amiss, even more so than usual.

"Ghouls, have you ever dreamed you went to school and everyone was staring at you, but you didn't know why? And then you passed a mirror and realized you were wearing nothing but leaves?" Venus babbled.

"Venus, was that your roundabout way of saying that you feel like everyone is staring at us?" Rochelle inquired.

"Yes, it was, and I didn't think it was that roundabout. I thought it was pretty obvious. Did you really need to double-check what I meant?" Venus pushed back.

"I'm a gargoyle. Do you really need to double-check that I need to double-check?"

"Bursting boilers! Everyone really is staring at us, and not in a good way. Maybe Rochelle was wrong? Maybe everyone's taken Spectra's comments to heart?" Robecca wondered aloud as a troll herded white cats past her in the hall.

"Ahh!" Clawdeen squealed as she threw a doll of doom from her locker onto the ground.

"Leave me alone!"

"Clawdeen, are you okay? You seem very agitated," Rochelle said honestly and then kicked the smashed doll of doom out of the way with her silver shoe.

"Well, clearly, they really do bring bad luck," Clawdeen prattled nervously as she stared at the ghouls and then hurried away.

As Clawdeen scurried down the hall, the trio looked at one another, silently noting the peculiar behavior.

"Good heavens! What in the name of the prickly pear is Hoodude doing?" Robecca asked as she pointed at the rag doll who was pressing his face firmly into one of the lockers.

"Hoodude? Are you okay?" Robecca asked sweetly.

"Uh . . . uh," Hoodude stuttered.

"To clarify, Robecca would like to know why you are pressing your face into the locker," Rochelle explained to the rag doll in her usual formal tone.

"I thought if I couldn't see you, you wouldn't be able to see me, but obviously I was wrong," Hoodude whined.

The soft-limbed boy then slowly pulled his head away from the locker and swallowed audibly.

"But why wouldn't you want us to see you?" Robecca inquired curiously.

"Please don't hurt Frankie," Hoodude whimpered before sprinting off, mumbling to himself.

"Will someone please tell us what's going on around here?" Robecca demanded, stomping her knee-high boot in frustration.

"Haven't you heard?" a smooth voice purred. "Or actually, haven't you *read*?"

218

The ghouls quickly turned around and discovered Toralei, iCoffin in hand and a smirk on her face.

"I assume you're referring to Spectra's blog, and to answer your question, yes, we read it," Rochelle replied, tapping her claws against her book bag.

"Oh, let me guess. You only read the *first* post? Don't worry, guys, I'd be more than happy to read the second one to you," Toralei said smugly. "'*According to an anonymous source, the 'they' referred to in the notes are none other than Robecca Steam, Rochelle Goyle, and Venus McFlytrap. In light of this information, I can't help but wonder if the whisper they supposedly saved us from was actually of their own doing.'*"

"An anonymous source?" Venus repeated in shock. "Who could that be?"

"Word on the street is that the anonymous

219

source is smart, stylish, and beautiful—the all-around *purrfect* ghoul," Toralei said, twitching her ears proudly.

"I know everyone's a bit rattled by the situation at Monster High, but remember, we're Frightingales. We must rise above fear and show others how to be brave," Draculaura declared poignantly to the room of jittery ghouls.

The stylish vampire was dressed in a pink-and-black plaid dress with a low-slung skull-and-crossbones belt. For as Draculaura saw it, if trouble was coming, she would face it head-on and well dressed.

"Thank you, Draculaura. And now I'd like to open the floor to suggestions on how we might help one another at Monster High as we face this unknown enemy," Frankie declared, fidgeting nervously with her strand of fangs.

"*Unknown?* How are they *unknown?* They're sitting right here," Toralei muttered loudly under her breath.

Venus, Rochelle, and Robecca stared apoplectically at Toralei, waiting for the other, more rational monsters to come to their defense. But as the seconds passed, they soon realized that it was not to be. On the contrary, other monsters actually joined Toralei in voicing suspicion.

"I always thought it was weird that they were the only ones not affected by the whisper," a young werewolf snarled loudly.

"They started the whisper, and then they took credit for stopping it? That's like writing the test, then boasting that you got an A. Totally unbelievable!" a vampire cried incredulously while shooting the trio a menacing look.

221

"Your dream of arriving at school *au naturel* suddenly seems almost pleasant in comparison to this place," Rochelle whispered to Venus and Robecca.

"Jeepers, you can say that again. . . ."

"Excuse me, Frankie, Draculaura? May I have the floor now?" Toralei asked as she walked to the front of the Arts and Bats room.

"Yes, but remember this is all about finding *constructive* ways to help one another. 'Constructive' being the key word, Toralei," Frankie responded, before taking a seat.

"Yeah, sure, Frankie," Toralei said before turning her attention to the crowd of ghouls. "As we all know, Monster High is currently facing some tough times. And when times get tough, monsters need to get tougher, smarter, and sneakier."

"Sneakier is not good, especially from her," Robecca mumbled to Rochelle and Venus as her

222

ears began to release small puffs of steam.

"Sometimes monsters need to protect them-selves, even from their own kind. Now obviously most of the monsters here are fine, but we can't let a few bad eggs ruin it for the rest of us," Toralei continued.

"The longer she talks, the worse I feel," Rochelle muttered, and then raised her cold granite hand to her forehead.

"And with that in mind, I propose we start the House for Unmonstrous Activities Committee, or HUAC, to which students will be able to report other classmates for unmonsterly behavior. Now, this shouldn't be an issue for anyone unless, of course, she has something to hide," Toralei finished while looking directly at Robecca, Rochelle, and Venus.

"This just got scary—very scary," Venus murmured, shocked by Toralei's suggestion.

223

"That's fine with me, but then again, I don't have anything to hide, except for my secret combination of hair-care products—that's confidential," Clawdeen explained as she caressed her silky locks.

"What is going on? I can't believe all you sensible ghouls are actually entertaining Toralei's suggestion. With all due respect to our werecat here, she has a bit of a checkered past when it comes to kindness," Frankie blurted out. "I know we're all scared, and we have good reason to be. But we're Frightingales; we have a moral code. We believe in honesty and community. We can't allow our fears to destroy who we are. And trust me, that's what will happen if we start spying on one another, reporting every little thing we hear or see. It's not right."

"Whatever, Frankie," Toralei growled. "Oh, and I've been meaning to tell you: Green's not your color."

"On that note, I think I'll bring this week's meeting to a close," Frankie said dejectedly, before collapsing onto her chair and placing her head in her hands.

Much like the parting of the Red Sea, the throng of monsters separated as Robecca, Rochelle, and Venus neared the door. Not wishing to touch the ghouls, even by accident, the crowd firmly pressed themselves against the craft-filled walls.

"Jeez Louise, we only just got settled at Monster High, and already we're outcasts," Robecca whispered glumly.

"Not exactly a good time, is it?" Venus replied, shaking her head, utterly incredulous at her peers' behavior.

"I find it most distressing that everyone outside

of Frankie has rushed to judgment. And absolutely no one has even bothered to research who Spectra's anonymous source is and whether he or she is even telling the truth," Rochelle barked as the sound of Cleo and Toralei fighting erupted behind her.

"Frankie, I wanted to let you know that I've decided to hold my own talent show tomorrow, separate from Toralei's, and I'm calling it Tomb Star," Cleo announced boldly.

"You do realize that mine will be a million times better than yours, don't you?" Toralei snapped.

"Ghouls, there can be only one show, and it's the Hex Factor. And it's tomorrow, so you're just going to have to find a way to work together," Frankie explained as patiently as possible.

Once they were a fair distance away from the others, Robecca, Rochelle, and Venus looked at one another and sighed, overwhelmed by what had just happened.

"We need to find out what Miss Flapper has to do with these messages," Venus said. "For our own sake as well as the school's."

"I thought it was awfully swell when they invited us to join the Frightingales, but now I sort of wish they hadn't," Robecca said sullenly.

"I must say, it's highly unpleasant being regarded as the enemy. Not that this comes as a great surprise to me," Rochelle said, before the sound of sloshing grabbed her attention.

"Ghouls! Ghouls!" Headmistress Bloodgood called out upon seeing Robecca, Rochelle, and Venus in the corridor.

"Headmistress Bloodgood, you're wetter than Miss Sue Nami," Robecca commented.

"This weather is simply ghastly. I went outside to check on one of the trolls who has taken to sleeping in a tree. He's in the midst of an identity crisis—I'm quite certain he thinks he's a squirrel. Normally I would just let him be, but with everything that's happening, we need all trolls on deck," Headmistress Bloodgood prattled on as she rung out her waterlogged outfit. "And this rain is just plain dreadful. Not to mention that I was nearly hit by lightning again."

"That would have been terrible. Your Muddled-Mind Syndrome would have returned with a vengeance," Rochelle speculated aloud.

"Oh, forget that. It's more that I wouldn't be able to say that lightning doesn't strike twice

anymore," Headmistress Bloodgood explained, and then shook her head at Rochelle as though it were the most obvious of answers.

"Headmistress, do you not recall that I explained this to you. Lightning—" Rochelle started, before being interrupted by Venus.

"Ro, I got this. Headmistress, on behalf of the entire student body, please do not go outside again until this storm passes once and for all."

"Very well, ghouls," Headmistress Bloodgood said as she touched her neck. "Oh dear, I think I have a leak; detachable heads are never *really* waterproof."

"Headmistress, I'm sure you've read the rumors about us," Venus interjected solemnly. "And, well—"

"Stop right there. Neither Miss Sue Nami nor I believe the gossip. You must understand, the students are scared. Actually, I am scared as well. We still haven't a clue who is behind all this."

"Didn't Miss Sue Nami speak to you about Miss Flapper?" Rochelle inquired.

"Oh, enough about Miss Flapper! I am an excellent judge of character, so you can trust me when I say that none of this has anything to do with that dragon. Honestly, I think Miss Sue Nami simply doesn't like Miss Flapper because she was popular in high school and Sue was not. . . ."

Then without so much as a good-bye, Headmistress Bloodgood wandered off, having completely forgotten that she was in the middle of a conversation.

"We need to get to the bottom of this, especially since it doesn't appear that Headmistress Bloodgood is looking in the right places," Venus said as her vines bristled.

"Should we ask Cy to help? Although, I haven't seen much of him lately. It's almost like he's avoiding me. You don't think he's avoiding me, do you?" Robecca asked Rochelle and Venus earnestly.

"No, of course not!" Venus replied vehemently—maybe a little too vehemently. "Cy would never do that to you."

"Unless, of course, he's like the rest of the school and thinks we're *them*," Rochelle interjected.

"Oh, this is sillier than a bee's sneeze in a strong breeze! Cy knows me; he knows all of us. He helped us defeat the whisper. I'm sure he's just busy, that's all. . . ."

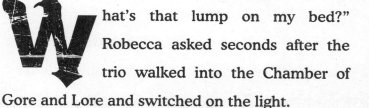

CHAPTER
fifteen

W hat's that lump on my bed?" Robecca asked seconds after the trio walked into the Chamber of Gore and Lore and switched on the light.

"Maybe it's Penny?" Venus offered as she began to unlace her pink boots, utterly exhausted from the long and emotionally taxing day.

"I'm afraid not. At the present time, Penny is seated on the windowsill staring angrily at Chewy, no doubt the result of an unwanted nibbling session. Perhaps it's time you look into getting Chewy a bone to gnaw on," Rochelle suggested,

233

before greeting her always-perky pet. "*Bonsoir,* Roux!"

"I hope I didn't leave my oiling can under here again. It took two straight hours of steaming to get that stain out last time," Robecca babbled to herself as she pulled back her mummy-gauze and werewolf-fur sheets. "Jeepers creepers! Someone left a giant egg in my bed!"

"An egg?" Venus repeated incredulously. "Let me guess: There's a giant chicken on the loose," she added.

Curiosity quickly got the better of Venus, prompting her to get up and look. The sight of the melon-size item on Robecca's bed gave Venus pause. It did, in fact, resemble an oversize egg. However, as Venus peered closer, she saw that it was not crafted out of shell but intricate spider threads in a delicate pattern.

"It's a spider's web, isn't it?" Rochelle inquired

as she climbed onto the bed to inspect it more closely. "There's something to all these webs. It doesn't make sense; it would take thousands of those little black spiders to produce the amount of threads found on campus, and yet we haven't seen one spider."

"It's true; outside of the ones in the dormitory hall, I haven't seen any," Venus replied as she picked up the webbed ball and studied it closely. "There's something inside."

"Good luck. This is like opening a seriously scary birthday gift," Robecca surmised.

"Why do I have to do it? It was found on your bed," Venus retorted and then put it down. "And let's not forget who pulled Rochelle from her webbed sleeping bag. . . ."

"*Vous êtes impossibles*! I'll do it," Rochelle said, reacting with palpable frustration.

"Well, you do have the perfect claws for opening things," Robecca added quietly as Rochelle tore open the webbing, revealing yet another doll of doom.

The jagged-edged figure's large black eyes seemed to stare ominously at Rochelle, momentarily shortening her breath. For one brief second, she was transported out of herself and to a place where she understood the others' irrational fears of the dolls and cats and such.

Wishing to literally destroy her fear, she

crouched down and slammed the doll against the floor. After pausing for one brief second, she resumed crushing the doll against the ground, banging it harder and harder until small bits of wood splintered off.

"Um, I'm pretty sure it's open," Venus stated wryly.

Rochelle then slammed the doll against the floor one more time.

"Oh, so it is," the granite-bodied ghoul replied softly.

"Is there anything you want to talk about?" Robecca asked Rochelle while shooting Venus a concerned look.

"What do you mean?" Rochelle responded in her normal matter-of-fact manner.

"You really let that doll have it," Venus said, pointing to the damaged figurine.

"Did I?" Rochelle questioned her friend.

237

"Um, yeah, you did. It was a little like gargoyle-versus-doll smack-down for a second," Venus countered with raised eyebrows.

Not wishing to admit her momentary lapse into the land of superstitious nonsense, Rochelle shrugged and set about opening up the doll.

Tucked inside was a small creased note wrapped in spiderwebs. After carefully removing the strands of webbing, Rochelle slowly unfolded the paper.

"'*They come tomorrow*,'" Rochelle read aloud, before sighing, clearly overwhelmed by the information.

"Tomorrow? I would have much preferred it said a month or even a year! I mean, we are definitely not ready for them!" Robecca whined with burgeoning hysteria and steaming ears.

"Robecca, grinding your gears is not going to help anything," Venus stated firmly.

"But they come tomorrow! And technically tomorrow is only a few hours away! Are they coming right at midnight? Or later in the day? The least they could have done was give us a specific time," Robecca prattled nonsensically.

"Give me that," Venus said as she grabbed the note, crumpled it into a ball, and walked over to Chewy. "Open wide, little friend."

And just like that the plant swallowed the balled-up wad of paper—whole.

"I never realized Chewy's talent for eating could be quite so helpful," Rochelle commented, genuinely impressed.

"Tomorrow, they're coming tomorrow," Robecca mumbled as she hugged Penny tightly, too tightly for the penguin's liking.

"What's so special about tomorrow?" Venus asked while staring at the half-demolished doll of doom.

239

"The Hex Factor . . ." Rochelle answered, looking at the calendar on her iCoffin.

As the outside world descended into meteorological chaos complete with hurricane-level winds, bouts of hailstones, and the continuing deluge of rain, Robecca, Rochelle, and Venus prepared themselves for what was sure to be an eventful day.

"Shouldn't we be warning people? Telling them what the note said?" Robecca asked as she walked out of the Chamber of Gore and Lore with Penny tucked tightly under her arm.

"In case you haven't noticed, we're social pariahs; no one is going to listen to us. Thanks to our 'anonymous' friend, aka Toralei, the whole school thinks we're the infamous *them*," Venus explained as she passed under the dormitory's webbed curtain. "And then there are the spiders; how do they fit in to all of this?"

"Maybe there's a spider whisperer among us?" Rochelle pondered aloud.

"It would take a small army of spiders just to carry the dolls and notes . . . never mind about the cats," Venus responded. "And thus far we haven't even seen a spider."

An unnerving clang and clatter greeted the three ghouls as they entered the main hall. With the wind continuing to rage outside, trees snapped, lawn furniture tumbled, and pretty much anything that wasn't bolted to the ground blew away.

While trying to ignore the jarring rattle of the storm, Rochelle spotted Trick and Treat and instinctually called out to them.

"Trick? Treat? Hello?"

But the trolls refused to answer; they wouldn't even look in her direction.

"Trick? Treat?" Rochelle called out louder.

"They're ignoring you, Rochelle. Don't take it personally. They're just scared," Venus explained.

"I shouldn't be surprised. Deuce e-mailed me this morning to say that Cleo no longer felt comfortable allowing him to tutor the trolls with me," Rochelle lamented with a hint of sorrow.

"It's surprisingly exhausting being unpopular," Venus said while stifling a yawn.

"Ghouls, excuse me?" Miss Flapper said. "Might I have a moment of your time?"

"Um, yeah, sure," Venus replied reticently.

"It seems you three are the target of a great deal of unfair gossip. And I think I know how you feel. After the events of last semester, a few monsters still look at me suspiciously, sure that I am up to no good. Why, a few have even followed me," Miss

Flapper said pointedly, her eyes filling with tears. "It's hard to handle the looks, not to take them personally. But remember, it's only fear clouding the monsters' judgment about you. And in those moments, those horrible soul-shaking moments, do you know what I remind myself? Everything eventually passes. Just focus on weathering the storm with as much grace and compassion as you can muster."

"Thank you, Miss Flapper," Robecca confessed honestly, clearly moved by the dragon's words.

"And on that note, my offer for tea and crones always stands," she said, before dabbing her eyes with a tissue and walking away elegantly.

"Definitely better than

Feral Streak. I mean, that was quite a performance," Venus muttered.

"Are you sure it was a performance?" Robecca inquired. "Is it possible that we misinterpreted what we heard about her plan? Maybe it was about her career plan here at Monster High?"

"*Boo-la-la*, Robecca. You don't really think that, do you?" Rochelle asked. "You can't possibly think that someone would climb through a crawl space to talk to her about getting tenure as a teacher?"

"No, I guess not. She just seemed so genuine, but like you said, she's a great actress," Robecca acquiesced.

"Interesting that today of all days, she pulls out all the stops, even tears, to try to win us over," Venus pondered. "She clearly wants to keep us off her trail."

"Who can tell me how to create the molecular

compound needed to make anti-fungus serum for pumpkin heads?" Mr. Hack asked the class as he rubbed his small elflike ears and waited for a volunteer.

In the back of the room, a small gray hand shot straight up in the air, eagerly waving side to side, desperate to garner Mr. Hack's attention.

"Dear me, you certainly are a glutton for punishment," Robecca said to Rochelle while shaking her head.

"Rochelle, it's with a heavy heart that I say this: Put down your hand. He's never going to call on you," Venus whispered to Rochelle.

"But I know the correct answer."

"And we know how much you love answers, but every student in here thinks we're a threat to the school. If he called on you, chaos would erupt in the classroom," Venus explained, just as a crackling sound came over the intercom.

"Miss Sue Nami, how do I turn this on?" Headmistress Bloodgood's voice barreled over the school's radio system. "Did I eat lunch today? I'm feeling awfully light-headed."

"That's because you have a leak in your neck, ma'am," Miss Sue Nami barked. "Oh, and the whole school is listening to this."

"Well, in that case . . . Hello, boys and ghouls, this is your headmistress speaking. I have just spoken with the sheriff, who informed me that the storm has knocked down at least twenty trees and utility poles on the road between here and town, so for the interest of all involved, Monster High shall be having its first-ever school-wide sleepover."

"Don't forget about the Hex Factor," Miss Sue Nami reminded Headmistress Bloodgood.

"But we shall still have the Hex Factor Talon Show, which, per the Toralei-Cleo Peace Summit, officially has no theme. Or perhaps it's nicer to think that each performer can create his or her own theme. . . ."

CHAPTER Sixteen

Small white candles lined the walkways in the Vampitheater, casting long and distorted shadows across the plush purple walls. Having lost electricity hours earlier, the school was now running solely on candlelight and ingenuity.

"Listen up, non-adult entities," Miss Sue Nami bellowed at the students as they filed into the candlelit Vampitheater for the Hex Factor. "Thank you for arriving already in your pajamas. Immediately following the show, you are to line up in the main corridor, at which time Ms.

Kindergrubber and I will pass out sleeping bags. As luck would have it, Ms. Kindergrubber has a rather well-stocked linen closet after teaching Home Ick for so many years."

"Hi, Robecca," Cy said meekly, trailing behind the ghouls as they made their way into the auditorium.

"Wow, I'm surprised you remember my name," Robecca huffed sarcastically.

"I don't understand . . ."

"Cy, you're even worse than an empty boiler!"

"I am?"

"I actually thought you were a true friend, but it turns out I was wrong. You disappeared the second everyone else did," Robecca said with steam pouring out of her ears, nose, and eyes.

"You're right, I did. . . ."

"And I deserve better than that from my friends," Robecca replied.

"But you see, that's just it. I don't want to be your friend."

"Cy Clops, you are the nastiest—"

"No, wait!"

The one-eyed boy then drew one deep breath as he prepared to say everything he so desperately needed to say as fast as possible.

"The only reason I stayed away from you was to get the courage to ask you to sit next to me during the show," Cy blurted out rapidly.

"Well, if that isn't the cat's pajamas, then I don't know what is," Robecca said, before leaning in and kissing Cy on the cheek. "I would be honored to sit with you."

Cy grinned like a pumpkin head and then followed the ghouls to their seats.

"All non-adult entities are to sit down!" Miss Sue Nami hollered from the stage.

"Is it just me, or are we the only ones in here

surrounded by empty seats?" Rochelle commented as she looked around the candlelit Vampitheater.

"Gee whiz, if I wasn't so thrilled about Cy still being our friend, that just might hurt my feelings," Robecca bubbled happily.

First onstage at the long-awaited Hex Factor Talon Show was none other than Three-Headed Freddie, who used his three mouths to juggle balls. While not the most interesting of acts, all the students appreciated the distraction. Well, except for Robecca, Rochelle, and Venus. With the knowledge that "they" would soon be arriving, the ghouls had no choice but to keep their eyes and ears peeled.

"Nice job, Freddie," Toralei droned sarcastically as she walked onstage at the end of his performance. "I've never tried juggling, but I'm sure if I did, I would be amazing, like a total superstar."

"Whatever, Toralei, everyone knows that mummies are the best jugglers," Cleo snapped as she pushed past the werecat. "Next up is Frankie Stein."

Frankie, dressed in all white and a large puffy chef's hat, wheeled a cart onto the stage. After adjusting her hat and apron, the green ghoul then cleared her throat and began singing.

"*I was working in the Creepchen late one night. When my eyes beheld a yummy sight. Two grated potatoes, one egg. A frying pan and a tummy to be fed. We did the hash. We did the monster hash. The monster hash. It was a graveyard smash,*" Frankie sang as she prepared hash browns onstage.

"Boys and ghouls!" Toralei called out as she ran onto the stage, interrupting Frankie's singing-

chef performance. "We really need to talk to you."
Just behind her, in high-heeled slippers, was an
equally distressed-looking Cleo.

"It's serious," Cleo added solemnly.

"If this is about the theme, I'm going to lose it,"
Venus muttered under her breath.

"While we were getting our makeup touched
up, a DeadEx zombie came in with a package.
And seeing as Cleo needs makeup way more than
I do, I signed for it," Toralei stated dramatically.

"And, of course, upon seeing that Toralei had
signed for a package, I immediately demanded
to see it," Cleo explained, wiping away tears.
"Understandably, I was a little concerned she was
trying to pull a fast one on me regarding the Hex
Factor theme."

"But of course I wasn't," Toralei interjected.

"Anyway, when I opened the package, I found
this large ball of spider threads, inside of which

was a letter,"
Cleo explained
as she unfolded a
piece of paper and started to read
it out loud. "*'We have taken your headmistress,
and we will not return her until you are properly
secured behind a locked wall. We do not wish to
encroach on your land. We will happily allow you
to keep all land currently inside the Salem city
limits. However, we no longer feel safe living so
close to creatures such as yourselves.'* That's all it
says."

Miss Sue Nami barreled onto the stage, water
spraying everywhere, and grabbed the letter from
Cleo's hand. As the Deputy of Disaster scanned
the note and slowly absorbed the shocking
information, the Vampitheater erupted into
hysterical chatter.

"It's the normies! *They* are the normies!"

"It's not Robecca, Rochelle, and Venus! It's the normies!"

"The normies are going to lock us up like animals, controlling our every move!"

"I don't believe this normie nonsense for one second. There hasn't been a major incident in the last half century between normies and monsters. There was that one with the dance, I guess, but that's it! So why would the normies suddenly take such a hostile stance? The answer is, they wouldn't," Venus whispered to Rochelle, Robecca, and Cy.

"You're right, but the question remains why does someone want us to think it's the normies?"

"Did you notice what Toralei said? That the note was covered in spiderwebs?" Robecca pointed out. "We need to follow the threads. There's something to all this webbing."

As Robecca, Rochelle, Venus, and Cy stealthily snuck out of the increasingly agitated

Vampitheater crowd, a shadow-drenched figure followed closely behind them. Once in the corridor, Venus motioned for Rochelle, Robecca, and Cy to follow her into the Mad and Deranged Scientist Laboratory for a bit of privacy.

"This whole normie nonsense is clearly about using our fears to control us. Deep down all monsters worry about normies. It's almost instinctual," Robecca mumbled as she took a seat on one of the lab benches. A slight steam erased the wrinkles from her pajama pants.

"I agree," Cy added. "All Cyclopes are raised to be weary of normies—not because they'll hurt us, but because they don't understand us."

A soft voice came from the doorway. "Excuse me? There's something I need to tell you."

"Spectra?" Venus said with obvious surprise.

"It-it has to do with my anonymous source," Spectra stammered reticently as she floated forward, her nightdress fluttering.

"You mean Toralei?" Venus interjected.

"Toralei? What are you talking about?" Spectra responded. "I've known Toralei for years, and trust me, I would never use her as an anonymous source. She'll say anything about anyone at anytime just to make herself feel superior."

"If it wasn't Toralei, then who was it?" Rochelle pressed Spectra.

"The monster was wearing a mask, but her delicate frame combined with one long red hair on her outfit led me to believe it was . . ." Spectra trailed off.

"Miss Flapper," Rochelle said with a sigh.

"That's the only reason I ran the piece. I thought my anonymous source was a teacher," Spectra explained, absolutely brimming with guilt.

"I understand," Robecca muttered, offering Spectra a compassionate smile.

"But that's not all. . . . I followed her . . . to the attic."

"The attic?" Rochelle repeated with surprise.

"Eek! What did you see?" Robecca asked impatiently.

"Well, at first I couldn't see anything. The whole place was covered in spiderwebs," Spectra prattled nervously.

"But?" Venus asked eagerly.

"But after cutting through layer upon layer of webs, I came upon some kind of office with a strange chart ranking monsters and the minutes from a secret meeting—I say 'secret' because everyone who attended was referred to by a code name. There was even a copy of Headmistress Bloodgood's schedule," Spectra said before pausing uncomfortably. "In the corner . . ."

"Deary me! What was in the corner?" Robecca exploded, steam pouring out her ears.

"A . . . a . . . a . . . spider."

"All that buildup for a little-bitty spider?" Venus huffed with palpable annoyance.

"I never said it was little," Spectra continued. "As a matter of fact, I'd say she was at least my height, if not taller."

"Hold on a second. Are you saying that there's a descendant of Arachne at Monster High?" Venus questioned Spectra with a confounded expression.

"Yes, I believe so," Spectra responded quietly, nodding her head.

"A descendant of Arachne has been living in the attic this whole time," Robecca mumbled to herself, clearly shocked by the news.

"Well, at least we know who visited Miss Flapper," Venus said to Robecca and Rochelle.

"No wonder we never saw any spiders. There was only one—one really big one," Robecca said with steam pouring out of her nostrils.

"Robecca, *s'il ghoul plaît*, don't oversteam yourself," Rochelle cautioned while putting her cold granite hand on Robecca's shoulder.

"What did the spider say when she saw you?" Venus inquired.

"She was asleep in her web," Spectra replied. "I was so afraid my chains might wake her, but luckily they didn't."

"*Pardonnez-moi*, but did you say there was a copy of Headmistress Bloodgood's schedule up there?" Rochelle asked Spectra.

"I did. Of course, at the time I didn't think anything of it, but as soon as I heard Headmistress Bloodgood had been kidnapped, I knew I needed to tell someone," Spectra offered quietly, still in awe from the shocking turn of events.

"But why us?" Robecca asked, her steam sputtering to a stop.

"I figured if you guys could stop a whisper, you're definitely Monster High's best bet at finding Headmistress Bloodgood."

"Deary me!" Robecca squealed. "Are we really her best bet? No offense to any of us, but that's a bit frightening."

"I know what you mean," Venus offered with a sigh. "And, I really wanted to just enjoy this sleepover!"

"Ghouls, you need to get it together, because it's not that we're just Headmistress Bloodgood's best bet; we're her only bet," Rochelle stated solemnly.

To be continued . . .

Don't miss the first book!

And keep a lurk out for the ghoulfriends' next adventure,

who's that ghoulfriend?

coming in autumn 2013!

ABOUT THE AUTHOR

As a child Gitty Daneshvari talked and talked and talked. Whether yammering at her sister through a closed door or bombarding her parents with questions while they attempted to sleep, she absolutely refused to stop chattering until finally there was no one left to listen. In need of an outlet for her thoughts, Gitty began writing, and she hasn't stopped since. Gitty is also the author of the series *School of Fear*.

She currently lives in New York City with her highly literate English bulldog, Harriet. And yes, she still talks too much.

Visit her at www.gittydaneshvari.com.